I was told, "everyone has a book in them"; when I retired, I tried out that statement. I enjoyed doing it and have had my first book published.

This has given me a great sense of satisfaction. Having created a cast of characters, I aim to use them in future stories.

Alice V Todd

THE DOCUMENT

AUSTIN MACAULEY PUBLISHERS™

LONDON • CAMBRIDGE • NEW YORK • SHARJAH

A CIP catalogue record for this title is available from the British Library.

ISBN 9781035834815 (Paperback)
ISBN 9781035834822 (Hardback)
ISBN 9781035834839 (ePub e-book)

www.austinmacauley.com

First Published 2024
Austin Macauley Publishers Ltd®
1 Canada Square
Canary Wharf
London
E14 5AA

I wish to thank John and Amanda Peters, Annette and Newton Moraes for their invaluable help; they were the cornerstone of the project, without which or whom, this book would not have been possible.

I acknowledge the input from the following books, periodicals and papers used as background material in this book:

A History of Agriculture—Franklin.

Astronomy Data Book—Robinson and Muirden.

Atlas of the Earth—Caxton.

Biographical Dictionary—W & R Chambers Ltd.

Catechism of the Catholic Church—G Chapman.

Chronicle of the Popes—P G Maxwell-Stuart.

Chronicle of the 20th Century—Chronicle Communications Ltd.

Contributors on the Internet:

Encyclopaedia of the Earth—Hutchinson.

Energy: The Solar-Hydrogen Alternative—J O M Bockris.

Father John Lee's Homily of 23 July 2017

Faster than the speed of light—Joao Magueijo.

Farming Technique from Prehistoric to Modern Times—G E Fossell.

Guinness Book of Air Facts and Feats—J & M Taylor and D. Mondey

Guinness Book of Astronomy—Patrick Moore.

Guinness Encyclopaedia of the Living World.

Medicine through the Ages—P. Mantin & R. Pulley

New Scientist—Reed Business Information Ltd.

Science and Invention—Cavendish Ltd.

State of the World—G. Gardner and P Sampat.

The British Broadcasting Corporation.

The Cambridge Encyclopaedia of Human Evolution.

The Evolving Continents—Brian Windley.

The Good News Bible—Collins.

The Guinness Book of Air Facts and Feats—J W R Taylor, M J H Taylor and D Mondey.

The Inventions that Changed the World—Readers Digest.

The Maidenhead Reference Library and its staff.

The Mill Hill Missions/ Maidenhead Missionaries.

The New Atlas of the Universe—Patrick Moore.

The New Jerusalem Bible—Darton, Longman & Todd Ltd.

The Origin of Humankind—Stephen Thomkins.

The Spectator.

The Tablet.

The Times Concise Atlas of the World.

The Weather Book—M Joseph Ltd.

The World's Great Religions—Collins (A "Life" Special Edition).

Table of Contents

Chapter One
Stonehenge

Christopher Allen is a very bright young man, almost twenty-two, and nearing the end of his second year at Cambridge. Reading both Math and Physics he is bright at the former and loves the latter because it reveals how the world and the universe work.

Christopher had been looking forward to a special, one-off lecture by Sir Michael Atiyah from Edinburgh University, who with Professor Singer in USA, had been developing an index theorem since the 1960s. It was now proving to be a practical bridge between mathematics and physics.

It had to be postponed at short notice due to a sudden indisposition, so this Wednesday afternoon was suddenly free. He grabbed at the chance to fulfil a long-held desire to see a summer solstice sunrise at Stonehenge. This opportunity was particularly good, it was the first year of the new millennium.

He was totally unaware that his visit to Stonehenge would be the critical turning point in the path that was his destiny.

He'd driven down to Maidenhead that afternoon to stay, with his parents and sister overnight. She'd just finished her A-levels and, subject to the results, had a place at St Mary's

Hospital Medical School, part of Imperial College. He'd had a pleasant, if shorter than average, evening with them, and an early night, setting his radio alarm for 2:30 the following morning.

He'd left the house before 3:00—made his way round the town centre, heading for Holyport, Bracknell and Junction 3 of the M3. It was dry and dark; the stars bright before they slowly dimmed with the very early twilight that presaged the dawn. He left the M3 at Junction 8, turning onto the A303 which would take him to Stonehenge. He'd made good time on the almost empty roads.

When the sky began to hint at lightness, the trees at the roadside became black silhouettes against this background, as did the few Alto clouds. As it became a little lighter, he noticed that a thin layer of mist had formed over the lower fields. A light breeze drifted tendrils of it across the road, through gaps in the hedges, giving an added sensation of speed as he sped through them.

When he'd come closer to Stonehenge, the traffic had got noticeably heavier. Police were evident, standing near their motorcycles or parked cars to control the traffic. There were many more mad people about, who also felt that the new millennium sunrise at Stonehenge would be worth seeing.

It was quarter past four when he was directed to drive past Stonehenge, continuing along the A303. He'd noticed bonfires out of the corner of his eye, as he passed. He'd also glimpsed what he assumed were flaming torches being tossed twirling into the air. He could vaguely discern an outline of the gathering crowd silhouetted in the firelight. Out of their midst towered the still-dark stone monoliths.

Temporary road signs displaying 'Solstice Parking' directed visitors to turn right onto a side road, and then off the road into a huge stubble field, a few hundred metres to the west of Stonehenge. It was by then, light enough to see the marshals directing cars into ever-increasing rows. He bumped his way over the rough ground, guessing there were probably a couple of thousand cars there already. Cars of every description from beat-up 'Beetles' to the latest 'Y'-registered Jag. He added his Golf GTI to their number.

He'd taken his anorak, locked the car and then traipsed over the stubble towards Stonehenge, going with the crowd. It was a cosmopolitan group of people of differing race and colour, the sophisticated and well dressed, to poorly turned out hippies. They'd merged into a column, all making their way towards the row clearly defined columns of stone in the ever-lightening dawn.

He noticed aircraft trails high in the sky, red like elements of an electric fire, lit by the sun he could not yet see. He'd arrived at the edge of the growing throng, disappointed at how the crowd shielded his view of the activity within the circle of stones. He was surprised to hear the buzz of two-stroke engines above the crowd's noise; suddenly discovering that three microlights and one paraglider made the noise, as they came into view.

Christopher had become fascinated with Stonehenge some years ago. The structure thought to be five thousand years old, aligned with both sunrise at the summer solstice and sunset at the winter solstice. There were also alignments with the moon. He reflected that astronomy was becoming more than just a hobby, recalling when his interest in astronomy had first been aroused. He was thirteen or fourteen, in church with his parents and sister. It was the first verse of a hymn that had captured his imagination.

O Lord my God, when I, in awesome wonder, consider all the worlds thy hand has made. I see the stars; I hear the rolling thunder, thy power throughout the universe displayed.

As he looked around, he thought some of the people might be sun-worshippers, possibly followers of Akhenaten, a past Egyptian king? Some maybe followed pagan rites of which he had no knowledge? Others perhaps were Hindus, believing the sun to be the eye of God looking down on the world? Presumably many were Druids who had somehow made Stonehenge theirs? The rest were probably people just like him, wanting to see a summer solstice sunrise in this unique place, on the 21st day of June, in the first year of the 21st century.

The gathering crowd had formed a massive throng of murmuring anticipation, watching the fire jugglers, chatting and waiting. Christopher had shivered with anticipation and the surprising early morning chill. He was thrilled that Stonehenge illustrated the fantastic precision of the solar system. Some five thousand years had passed since Stonehenge was first laid out, yet, when the first rays of the sun cleared the horizon, they would once again shine upon the Altar Stone—still precisely aligned.

It was 4:51 BST when the first rays of the sunrise shone above the north-eastern horizon. They passed the Heel stone, on between the two Sarsen stones, then between the two Blue stones, which were the open end of the horseshoe of

Trilithons. Finally, with the precision of ages past, they cast their light once more upon the Altar Stone.

At that moment, Christopher suddenly seemed to be in another place. It was as if a magical time machine had transported him to an ethereal, timeless location. It was truly regal. A great king was seated on a throne, the like of whom he'd never seen. He was no ordinary king; his face was like an arrangement of the finest jewels. He was dressed in white with splashes of red, yellow and gold, he shone bright like the sun. An unusually beautiful rainbow that containing every hue of green, encircled the king. It was a sight that filled him with awe and wonder.

The king was seated before a myriad beings dressed in white, they stretched as far as the eye could see. They were singing of their king's greatness—paying homage—happy and at peace in his presence. However in one small part of this massive throng he noticed a disturbance. He knew, as if by clairvoyance, that a group of beings were jealous of the king's great power. Their leader had been spreading discord, carrying others with him.

There was no trial, simply autocratic decisiveness. The rebel leader's attire turned black—the garments of his followers likewise. The great king spoke to them in a booming voice of great anger that sounded like thunder.

"You are to be banished forever to the farthest place. I will create a vast gulf between us, so deep and so wide, that you will never be able to return. Be gone from this place!" The king was absolutely awesome.

The rebels were ejected instantly—like a bolt of lightning—they were gone. The king then spoke to the assembly in a voice now devoid of anger.

"I will replace the fallen angels with new loyal beings who will not rebel—they will have earned their place with me. Those that do not will forever join the rebels without ever setting foot in my kingdom."

Just as suddenly, the vision vanished and Christopher became aware of his surroundings once more. He was astounded that no time appeared to have passed, for the rim of the glowing sun was barely above the horizon, just beginning to bathe Stonehenge in the new light of day.

Christopher watched the glorious sunrise, wondering at the vision he'd seen, when a gust of wind came, causing a sheet of paper to wrap itself against his leg. He bent down, picked it up, roughly folded it and stuffed it in his anorak pocket.

As he stood erect once again, he became aware of a lovely redhead near him. He could have sworn she was not there before he bent down—he surely would have noticed? She was the most beautiful young woman he'd ever seen. At twenty-one, he'd already noticed quite a few, but they were as nothing as compared to her! He was transfixed, stunned by her appearance as she turned and smiled at him. His heart seemed to miss a beat—she was really gorgeous. She was tall and lithe, almost as tall as his five-foot-eleven frame. She looked slender and well dressed—her finest feature, a wonderful head of titian hair, shining in the light of the sun. It framed the fair skin of her face, a kind mouth and deep blue eyes. In that moment he was speechless, knowing in his heart that she deserved to be the woman in his life.

He forgot about the sunrise, realising that if he didn't say something, she might be gone from his life forever? He introduced himself falteringly, saying, "My name is Christopher; I can't understand how I didn't see you earlier."

In an American accent, she said, "Hello Christopher, my name's Emmanuelle, Emmanuelle Theurgy. It's a bit of a mouthful, but I am not keen on either Emma or Manny; so most people call me Thea for short."

"Hello Thea," he said, shaking hands, "it's a real pleasure to meet you. I was thinking about the marvels of the universe and the solar system in particular earlier, I must have been miles away in some kind of daydream or reverie, perhaps that's why I didn't see you?"

"Well, it's a large crowd; there must be thousands here. I'm thin, I'm easily missed sideways on," she said with a smile, teasing him just a little.

"You're not thin, you are just right, in fact you are beautiful."

Thea went slightly pink, then so did he. He realised he'd blurted-out his inner thoughts, embarrassing both of them.

"I'm sorry, I didn't mean to embarrass you," he said, "What I really meant to say was that I'd like to get to know you."

Glancing momentarily at the burgeoning sun he added, "I've wanted to come here to see this for a long time, astronomy's my hobby, but I never dreamt it would be surpassed by my meeting someone like you. What brought you here?"

"I came at my father's suggestion, he told me that the summer solstice sunrise at Stonehenge was unique and should not be missed; in fact it's magnificent—we're lucky it's such a fine morning."

Then, with a similar teasing smile, she added, "but now it seems I came to meet you."

Not knowing how to respond to that statement, he asked, "Where are you from Thea?"

"I'm from Boston, but I'm living in Hammersmith at the moment. I'm over here doing social research."

"I'm from Maidenhead," Christopher said, "but I'm up at Cambridge at the moment—neither is all that far from Hammersmith, so maybe we could meet up…"

With a winning smile, he said, "I've just had a better idea. If you're willing; it's a bit of a cheek as we've only just met, but I've got to get back to Cambridge by eleven for a lecture. I planned to stop on the M3 for breakfast on my way back, would you like to join me by any chance?"

"I'd love to, I didn't have any breakfast either before I left."

"Great," said Christopher, "let's do that."

They stood in companionable silence for a while watching the sunrise, but their minds in something of a turmoil. Christopher's interest in the sunrise was rapidly waning, his thoughts becoming centred on the idea of getting to know Thea.

Thea had liked Christopher instantly and was wondering if he was the man that she'd been waiting for?

Once the sun was clear of the horizon, starting its climb into the sky, Christopher noticed that the black Alto clouds of early dawn had now turned white in the morning sunlight. He was excited by the prospect of having breakfast with Thea.

The sunrise having finally lost its attraction, he looked at his watch and said, "If we leave now Thea, we'll have plenty of time for a leisurely breakfast, I'm starving, how about you?"

"Yes, let's do that, we've seen what we came to see, I sure could use a coffee and breakfast."

They noticed that they were among the first to leave, as they traipsed back to the car park. They were preoccupied with their own thoughts, neither quite knowing how to start a conversation.

Christopher's mind was in a whirl, Thea was really lovely; instinctively he felt she was the girl he was going to marry. He briefly recalled the strange vision that had played in his mind as the first rays of the sunrise shone on the Altar Stone. He also remembered picking up a piece of paper that caught his leg and then seeing Thea for the first time as he stood up.

He wondered at the fate that had brought him to Stonehenge?

Thea was strangely aware of her life's purpose—she was preoccupied by the question—was Christopher the one she was to help and if so, in what way?

As they got closer to the field full of cars, Thea asked if he would give her a lift. She explained that she'd been dropped off earlier by a friend.

He was delighted to have her company on the drive and more than happy to open the door of his Golf GTI for her. She further explained her friend worked for one of the courier companies, she had to deliver a package to Exeter by 7:00, and would pick her up on the way back. She'd phone her on her mobile later to change the pick-up point.

Christopher had pulled out of the temporary car park onto the side road, then turned eastward on the A303. The conversation was a little stilted at first, neither knowing the other's interests. She admired the wonderful views of the English countryside as he drove; he talked of his life in Cambridge. She explained that this was her first visit to England and Europe, but they also lapsed into short periods of companionable silence.

He vividly remembered the mystical vision at sunrise— his awe and wonder as he beheld the mighty king. The king was not a Druid, nor a sun god, of that he was sure, but he felt it was some kind of religious experience nonetheless. It had touched his soul. He was raised as a practicing Anglican, but had lapsed during his first year at university. He now felt he would reflect more deeply on this dream-like 'religious' experience.

He remembered the paper caught against his leg, his aversion to litter, so putting it in his anorak pocket. His heart leapt as he thought about Thea who now sat at his side.

It was a little before six as they passed Junction 4 on the M3, then slowed for the turning into Fleet services. They were pleased to be in each other's company as they walked into the restaurant, got some breakfast and sat down.

As they ate, Thea told Christopher about her European assignment. The company she worked for supplied both government and industry, in the USA, with detailed background information of almost any country in the world. He in turn explained what he was studying at Cambridge; his aspiration was to become an astrophysicist under Stephen Hawking.

When they'd finished breakfast they exchanged mobile phone numbers before they parted, with a kiss on the cheek, agreeing he would phone to arrange a meeting in the near future.

Leaving the Fleet services, Christopher thought about Thea. In spite of their short acquaintance, she seemed to be a lovely young woman, one in whom he would feel confidant; would be proud to take home. Strangely, he realised, his attraction to her was not lustful, but something deeper, more respectful, he wanted to spend time with her, getting to know her better.

His feelings were unlike those in the first of his two years at university, when a female student had a crush on him. He'd been flattered, had first kissed, then indulged in heavy petting, finally becoming intimate having spent numerous nights of passion with her, it was now over.

He was not promiscuous, his upbringing frowned on fornication, but she seemed nice and he had lusted after the experience. He found it had badly distracted him from his studies. So he now felt the time for real love would come when he was set on his career and in a position to make a firm commitment. His first priority was, and would remain, his studies.

But Thea was different, there was something uniquely attractive about her, it wasn't just her looks. Emmanuelle was rather a mouthful. Theurgy an odd surname, but he'd heard of Americans with much stranger names? Her attitude was self-confident, slightly teasing, even at their first meeting. He recalled her directness and his surprise, when she'd said, "I came to meet you." She seemed to like him, but there was something reserved about her; maybe she was purposely mysterious? She seemed calm and at peace with herself; was well spoken, seemed to be modest, and he undoubtedly wanted to know more. His thoughts were kaleidoscopic, he liked her, he liked her a lot. No doubt his thoughts would clarify when he got to know her better.

He wondered again at how suddenly she'd appeared, almost at his side? The more he thought about it, the more he felt sure she was not there before the sunrise. She was so stunning that he would surely have noticed! It was as if she'd materialised from nowhere without him seeing, he was glad she had—she really was quite special.

Early that evening, before he got down to his studies, he remembered the screwed-up paper in his anorak pocket. He fetched it to throw in the waste bin, but its feel made him curious to see what it was. As he flattened it out on the table he became sure that it was no ordinary piece of paper, its quality was superb. The typeface, or writing, he couldn't tell which, was clear, but his curiosity was thwarted because it was in some unknown foreign language.

He'd been ready to discard it, but now, his curiosity aroused, he folded it and put it in his wallet. Such quality surely meant it was worthy of a little investigation. He would search out one of the university professors who might be able to translate it for him.

On impulse he decided to phone Thea, he wanted to share the mystery with her. He looked out her number and dialled.

"Hello Thea, its Chris."

"Oh hello Chris, what a nice surprise. Did you have a good journey back to Cambridge?"

"Yeah, I got back with half an hour to spare—how about you?"

"Fine, I was back at 9.30; I didn't have to wait long after you left."

"I've been thinking," said Chris, "Maidenhead's a lot nearer than Cambridge, I'll be home in ten days' time for the summer break, how about we meet up then?"

"That sounds great, I'll look forward to it, but my work schedules a bit in the air at the moment. I'm in the early stages of my assignment, can I phone you once I've got things settled?"

"Of course you can, it's the same with me in a way, I'm not sure what my parents have planned, so I'll check, then we can firm up."

"It sounds as if your parents will be on holiday too?"

"Well, sort of, they're school teachers; dad teaches math and mum religious education, so they get quite a bit of time off in the summer. What about you and your parents?"

"Its parent, in the singular, there's only my father, he's something of an antiquarian, he'll take time off when I go back for a week or two."

A short silence followed, Chris not quite sure what to say next. But just before the silence lengthened into embarrassment, he remembered the reason for the call; the curious note he'd found.

"When we were at Stonehenge this morning, you may have seen me pick up a piece of paper that had blown in a gust of wind. I'd put it in my pocket to throw away. I remembered it a short while ago and took a look before I threw it away. It's quality paper, and what's on it looks like an ancient script. It made me curious, so I decided to keep it and see if one of the lecturers can recognise it. He might even be able to translate it, if I'm lucky?"

"It sounds interesting, I'd be curious too. Why don't you send me a photocopy, I'll contact my father and see if he can help."

"Would you Thea, that would be great, where shall I send it?

"To my flat, it's in a big paper… right, go ahead."

"Seven eighty-nine, South End House, Fritzjames Ave, W14 1HZ

"Great, I'll post a copy in the morning. You're sure your dad won't mind?"

"No, he's missing me already, he's always pleased to hear from me, I'll scan it and email it to him."

It was about four days later when Thea called.

"Chris, it's Thea. I got a message back from my father, it's Aramaic, he also sent me some notes about the language. It came into being before the Christian era more than a thousand years BC. It became the language of the Jews when they came to Palestine. Jesus preached Aramaic, and parts of the Old Testament were written in it."

"I've heard of it, but no wonder I couldn't recognise it. So what does it say?"

"I don't know yet, Chris, he said it's odd, he wants to consult with a couple of colleagues to be sure it's translated correctly."

"Well, you got a lot further than I did. I found a professor who thought he recognised the script, but wasn't sure, and certainly couldn't translate it."

"When exactly are you going to Maidenhead, Chris?"

"This coming Thursday, how about we meet up on Saturday?"

"That'll be good, I'm off to Brussels on Sunday. I'd like to come out to Maidenhead if you don't mind. It'll be nice to get out of town and see something new and get some fresh air."

"I like that idea. It'll be nice to show you around the area; will you be driving down?"

"Yes, I don't need a lift this time."

"Well, come down the M4, then come off at Junction 7— Slough West and get on the A4, when you get to Maidenhead bridge over the Thames, ask anyone for Boulters Lock. It's well known, I'll meet you there."

"Would about eleven be ok?"

"Yeah, there's a small park by the lock, I'll ask mum to make us a picnic, and then we can walk along the river or whatever, afterwards."

"That sounds lovely, just what I need, it will be nice to see you again."

"Bye, Chris, and God bless."

Christopher had already told his mother and father, over the phone, about the piece of paper he'd found at Stonehenge. Once he was at home, he showed it to them and his sister, explaining how his curiosity was aroused.

He'd left telling them about Thea until he was home, he knew they would worry that she might distract him from his studies. He explained they'd literally only met for few minutes at Stonehenge because he had to get back to Cambridge. They had a couple of phone calls since, about the document, because her father had identified the language, it was Aramaic and he was translating it. He told them he'd arranged to meet Thea at Boulter's Lock Park on Saturday, when, hopefully, she would have the translation. He asked his mother if she'd make them a picnic lunch.

"What did you say her surname was?" asked his mother.

"Theurgy," he repeated. "Emmanuelle's a bit of a mouthful; she doesn't like Manny or Emma, so she likes to be called Thea for short. She's American working in Europe for a while, but I don't know much about her."

"It's an unusual name, I've heard it somewhere before, but in a different context, it'll come back to me."

That evening Christopher was reading a physics book in his father's study, which he now let him share when he was home. His mother came in and said, "Chris; there's something odd about Thea."

"What do you mean, odd, mum, you've never met her."

"Sorry Chris, I worded that badly, it's not Thea herself, but her name. I knew I'd heard it before—it's just come back to me—where's the dictionary?"

Chris took it from a shelf and handed it to his mother.

Turning the pages, she then said, "Yes, it's here, Chris—Theurgy—the intervention of a divine or supernatural agency in the affairs of man."

I must have heard it during teacher training. What makes it more intriguing is if you combine it with her Christian name, I looked it up, there's a verse in St Matthew's Gospel which says, "A virgin will become pregnant and have a son, and he will be called Emmanuel." (Which means 'God is with us'.)

As she read the meaning of Theurgy and then told him the meaning of Emmanuel, a small shiver went up and down his spine. "I see what you mean, mum. I thought her name was strange when she first told me, it's certainly food for thought."

He stored his mother's revelations with his private thoughts concerning Thea, and the strange events at Stonehenge. He couldn't make sense of it yet, but given time, he thought, things will surely clarify.

Christopher was early, so he went into the park to decide where would be the best place to picnic? As he did so the vision of the great king flashed into his mind and was gone. Then, to his surprise he saw Thea, she was already there, sitting on a bench.

As he walked towards her, she saw him, got up, smiled and said, "Hallo Chris, I allowed too much time, and I didn't want to be late, so I decided to sit and enjoy the sunshine."

Her appearance caused him to forget about the translation of the document and about the meaning of her names. Taking her hand he said, "Hallo Thea" kissed her on the cheek saying, "you look wonderful, even lovelier than I remember. You found it easily I hope?"

"Yes, I stopped near the bridge to ask the way, as you suggested, then came straight here. Let's walk shall we? I haven't explored the park, I didn't want to miss you, but I'd like to stretch my legs after the drive."

As they strolled around the park they discovered more about each other as they talked. Thea was a Catholic, rising twenty-three. She had grown up in a place called Towson in Maryland, not far from Baltimore.

She got her BA in business administration at Radcliffe College, the female part of Harvard, last year. She pointed out a coincidence; it's located in a part of Boston called Cambridge.

She was the only child, and after her mother died, her father wanted a complete change. He'd visited her and took a liking to Boston and New England when he came for an interview. His new job was in the Peabody Museum of Archaeology, also part of Harvard University.

She was then in her final year and they had found a suitable home in Somerville, an outer suburb of Boston. It was convenient for both the university, and the museum; not far from the coast. She'd done her best to make it a home for her father, while she completed her final year.

Having got her BA, she was about to start looking for a job when a one-off opportunity arose.

She'd accepted it, thinking like it was a gap year, for the experience and the chance to travel round Europe. She was due to finish in December, probably a little before Christmas. Christopher then told her, he was born and bred in Maidenhead. At eleven, he went to Desborough School, where his father Eugene was head of math. He had a sister Helen who was a couple of years younger than him.

His mother Pat taught religious education at Newlands, a girl's school in Maidenhead where his sister had been. She'd just completed her A-levels and hoped for a place at Imperial College in London; she wanted to become a doctor. She also hoped that the college would agree a gap year before she started, she wanted to travel. In fact she planned to spend six months working at an orphanage in Pattaya, about seventy miles south of Bangkok, in Thailand. Their parents sponsored a child there; they had done for a number of years.

They stopped at Christopher's car and got the picnic basket from the boot, taking it to their chosen spot for lunch. As they did so he was telling her that both sets of grandparents were farmers. Those on her father's side had been killed in a tragic car accident a few years ago. As his father was the only son and not interested in farming, it had been sold, with a fifth left in trust, to both him and his sister when they reached eighteen. His parents were still farming in Oxfordshire, although they were getting close to retirement now.

Thea told him she'd already spent time in some capital cities of Europe so far this year, doing her research. She still had Zurich, Brussels, Paris and Madrid to do. She would probably have to do some revisits towards the end. Each visit had lasted one or two weeks, getting copies of government reports, statistics, research papers and things like that. It was proving interesting, with the opportunity for some limited sightseeing.

They were now talking like they'd known each other for years—easy in each other's company. They were just finishing their picnic when Thea said, "Oh! We've forgotten all about the reason for my visit, the document you picked up. I got my father's translation yesterday evening, he's very intrigued and wants to know how it came into your possession? You're going to have some difficulty in believing what it says," and taking it from her handbag she handed it to him.

The Document

Christopher took the proffered sheet from her with a feeling of wary anticipation, he then carefully unfolded the page and began to read:

Location:

- *Galaxy—Sp 615,761,893—MW*
- *Star—CC27K*
- *Planet—03—4.110 /1—6/15—M21C*

Current Status:

- *Satan licensed—Soul yield falling.*

Twenty-Third Phase (Start 1960-Finish 980)

Remedial Actions Decreed:

- *Increase agricultural output to ten billion level.*
- *Raise vulnerability awareness.*
- *Environment—materials—energy.*

After a suitable period:

- *Initiate new energy source.*
- *Apply medical knowledge limitation.*
- *Provide additional communications capability.*
- *Permit inter-planetary travel only.*
- *When fully prepared—make final call to conversion.*

On his first reading, Christopher's comprehension was limited, he just thought—Wow! Seeing what he assumed was this world, referred to in such a forthright manner, came as something of a shock.

He read it more slowly for a second time, the enormity of its content still barely sinking in. If true, it was almost beyond belief.

"It's got to be a hoax," he said, "a few dozen sheets dropped in the crowd for a laugh, it can't be real can it? I never imagined it would be anything quite like this! What do you think Thea?"

"Well, Chris, I've only had a little more time to think about it than you. I had the same reaction initially. But then I started to take it more seriously, for three reasons. First there is the unusual and little-known language—whoever did it would have to have been a real scholar? Second, the undoubted quality of the paper you talked about—would a hoaxer use such quality? Incidentally, I'd love to see the original. Finally, the reference to the twenty-third phase, as if it's part of a continuing process? To my mind, a hoax doesn't fit with the sophistication required to do this; the two just don't go together somehow?"

"I agree with your father, it's certainly intriguing—I'll have to think about it a lot more. I've got the holiday in front of me, maybe I'll think of something I can do to verify it, one way or the other?"

"Just as I was going off to sleep last night, or perhaps I had already fallen asleep and it was a dream, I don't really know? I saw a clerk, with many, many files in front of him, one for each inhabited planet in the universe, I think. He was handed a sheet, with God's edicts listed on it. I saw it as it was being filed—it looked like the one in your possession, I'm somehow sure it was the twenty-third sheet in that particular folder."

"Your mind must have been working on it subconsciously, it does read and look like a sheet from a loose-leaf folder. I'll show it to my parents and see what they think? It's difficult, but let's try and forget about it for now, I promised to show you some of Maidenhead. If we pack up and put this stuff back in my car, we can start with a walk along the river."

"Yes let's, it's such a lovely day. I've been looking forward to it."

"What do you think dad?"

"Well, it reads rather like a management summary, it's a kind of memo. It's issuing orders, giving instructions. It might be a practical joke—some wag dropped a few of them at Stonehenge for a bit of a laugh. If it's real, its mind blowing, it hardly bears thinking about."

"That was my first reaction. But you've seen the original, its top quality. Thea made a good point; the sophistication needed to produce it seems inconsistent with a hoaxer."

"She could be right; it's certainly weird. I wonder what mum and Helen will make of it when they get back?"

The first thing his mother said when she came home was "how did your meeting with Emmanuelle go?"

"Oh fine, Thea was already there when I arrived. We strolled round the park for a bit, then had our picnic, which was really good thanks. We chatted about each other's background, then the document, and finally we walked along the river for a while, before she had to go back."

"I hope you didn't try to discuss her name did you!"

"Of course not, mum, I'm not stupid, I hardly know her."

"Good, so what do you think, now you've spent a bit time with her?"

"She's really nice. She's got a BA in business administration at Harvard and is doing a research job that's taking her round Europe. She's off to Brussels tomorrow, that's why she had to leave, to get her stuff ready. The job ends in December, she'll be going back to America for Christmas."

Then she asked, "Had her father sent a translation of the document?"

"Yes, he said he was intrigued by it—and you'll both be astounded; dad and I were."

"Where is it Chris?" said Helen, "go and get it, don't keep us in suspense, let's read it." So he fetched the translation for them.

After a pause his mother said, "This isn't real is it? It's a put-on surely?" She then passed it to Helen.

After a further pause… "Gosh, I see what you mean—it really is quite something, I wonder who on Earth could have dropped it?"

"I don't suppose we'll ever find out," their father said.

"I think it could be real," said his mother, "but if it is, its content's quite astounding."

"But if it's real, who lost it, or was it deliberately dropped?" Helen remembered Chris's explanation of why he picked it up, and added, "Did Chris pick it up by accident or design?"

"I think that's getting a bit too deep for now," said Gene, "We could speculate forever without reaching a conclusion."

That's how it was left until the evening, each with their own thoughts, wondering about its origin and its content?

During their evening meal the subject naturally arose once again. It started when Gene said, "I think the first thing you have to decide Chris is whether you are prepared to act as if the document's genuine or not. You either forget about it because you're convinced it's a hoax, or you think there's a chance it might be real and try to work out what it means?"

Pat was intrigued because religion was her subject. "I think he should assume it's real," she said. Chris's got nothing to lose. We're on holiday, if it is real, we might be able to help, we might make some kind of sense out of it between us. I'd like to see what we could discover?"

That had not been too far from Christopher's thoughts either. "A number of things lead me to think it could be real," he said, "but it might be a hoax; I need to think it through. For example, it's addressed to what I assume are God's people, whoever they are? Surely they would not be visiting a pagan monument or festival."

"Oh I don't know Chris," said Pat. "I seem to remember Stonehenge was started around three thousand years BC. We don't know what Bronze-age man's religion was, it's only assumed it's was based on sun worship? The only religion we know about of that time, with that theme, is Hinduism, and that was in India. Secondly, God used a star to communicate with the three wise men when Christ was born, if you remember—so why not the sun, is just another star. Stonehenge might not have been built for sun worship at all; it could have been a form of celestial clock to establish the seasons. Going way out, as you might say, it could even have been built as a portal to heaven, for all we know—a bit like the pyramids?"

Thoughts of his vision flashed into Christopher's mind as his mother talked of a portal to heaven. He needed to think about that too, so many strange events were encircling him?

Helen chipped in; "The Old Testament's full of stories where God intervened in the affairs of mankind. What I find incredible, is the thought that if the document's genuine, the hand of God, even today, is involved in the affairs of mankind?"

As Helen said this, Christopher thought again of the meaning of Thea's names. His sister hadn't been in his father's study when his mother explained their meaning. Unexplained events were piling up, challenging his mind to find a resolution, suddenly things seemed very odd indeed?

Gene said in response to Helen's remarks "that's just what we hope to find out, one way or the other—is the document for real or not?"

They were relaxing after their evening meal; Gene was looking at the translation once again. "I think we can forget the first two lines of the document for the time being, I think it's reasonably safe to assume the galaxy reference is the Milky Way, although I'm surprised, we're in the hundreds of millions. Similarly, with the planet reference, whatever it means, it's us, planet Earth."

"Yeah," said Chris. "The Earth is the third planet from the sun; Mercury and Venus are first and second. That could account for the 03."

"That's a valid point Chris," his mother said, "that's the first step in understanding the document, whether it's real or a hoax. In spite of what your father just said, you and your father are good at numbers, I think you should concentrate on the numbers first."

"That sounds like good advice," said Chris. "We might begin to break into its meaning through that route."

Christopher was preoccupied for the rest of the evening, not just with the document and what it might mean, but about the juxtaposition of the three other events that surrounded it. All four came in such quick succession.

First was what he perceived as the trigger, the fresh light of the rising sun when it touched the Altar Stone.

Then came the picture of a king in fantastic surroundings. The wonderfully glorious singing of beings he could not identify. Yet there was discord, the banishing of a leader and his followers. The memory now felt special, religious, even precious. He felt privileged to have seen it, could it really have been a vision? He could hardly admit it to himself, let alone speak of it to others, so he had instinctively kept it to himself.

Then there was the very strange document that came into his possession. Was it just a chance event—he'd almost thrown it away at one point? Taken as part of the whole, he now tended to think it could be real, was it meant for him, if so why?

Finally, there was the most intriguing event of all—the sudden appearance of Emmanuelle Theurgy and his reaction to her. He just had to know her, felt compelled to do so there and then! He had enjoyed his time with her. His feelings were not lustful, but he simply felt he wanted to spend time with her, listen to her, be in her presence—it was all so confusing.

He felt he'd been thrown in the deep end at Stonehenge, thrown into a pool he didn't understand, now he was struggling to swim. He must try to understand, address the questions logically and in so doing reach a valid conclusion. He would take a step at a time to resolve each question the events posed. Additionally, he would spend what time he could with Thea, she was part of the whole, of that he was sure. But at holiday's end, the events resolved or not, he would put his university studies back at the top of his agenda.

Chapter Two
Numbers

Christopher sat contemplating the first line of the document. If the document was meant for him, logic dictated that it would be addressed in a way he could understand.

If this was the case then in the Galaxy line under location—Sp 615,761,893—MW—the Sp could stand for Spiral, as the Milky Way is a spiral galaxy like Andromeda, and MW could stand for Milky Way. He found that once he applied his mind to it the task proved easier than expected.

The number on the document, almost six hundred and sixteen million, was a huge figure. He knew from his reading that within the universe there were thought to be more than a million, million galaxies. This number could represent the six hundred and sixteen millionth spiral galaxy, or, more probably, the six hundred and sixteen millionth galaxy to be formed? It could even be another way of numbering altogether, he doubted that it was necessary?

Following the logic of his thoughts, he had a feeling he now knew the meaning of the next line, Star—CC27K. He pulled out the astronomy book his parents had given him for Christmas some years ago. Turning to the chapter on the formation of the solar system, he found what he was looking for. In summary it said—'Our sun was created from a massive explosion, about five billion years ago. It was thrown onto the inner edge of one of the arms of our galaxy called Carina Centauri. It is located about twenty-seven thousand light years from the centre of the galaxy.' It was as he recalled—the description accounted for the CC and the 27K.

Coming to the third line he became stuck. He had instinctively understood—Planet—03 coming after Mercury and Venus, but the rest meant nothing. He thought long and hard over—4.110 / 1—6 / 15—M21C. The nearest he got was that the Earth had been formed four point six billion years ago, and that wasn't 4.11 billion? As for the rest he had no idea whatever. He finally decided to leave it, as it was almost time for lunch, in the hope that things would clarify when he returned to it.

After lunch, Helen, having just come into her inheritance and accompanied by her father, had gone into town to book a ticket to Thailand for mid-September. She was going to have a two-week, two-centre holiday, in Chiang Mai and Bangkok before starting at the orphanage; she planned to be in Pattaya for October 1st. She booked an open return, on her father's advice, just in case she didn't get the A-grades she needed, couldn't get agreement for the gap year, or in the event that she wanted to leave the orphanage earlier than planned.

Christopher and his mother were sitting in the garden, chatting over a lazy after-lunch coffee, when he raised the topic of the document. He told her he was working on the assumption that the document was genuine. He also said he was determined to solve the meaning of the document, during the holiday, if he possibly could. He then told her about his thoughts on the first section—the Galaxy, Star and Planet.

"I guessed that's what you were doing," she said.

He explained he was fairly happy with the first two, as a working hypothesis, but he was stuck on the third—the planet, so he'd decided to leave it for the moment. He also intended to leave the next section—Current Status, to concentrate on to the further numbers, as she had recommended.

"While I've left Current Status for the time being, could you spend some time thinking about it," he asked.

"Is that the line that says Satan Licensed and Soul Yield Falling?"

"Yes, that's the one. While I might get somewhere with the numbers, you're much better than me when it comes to religion and the bible."

"Flattery will get you everywhere," she said laughingly. "Yes, I'll see what I can come up with."

Christopher sat thinking about the line, which read— Twenty-Third Phase (Start 1960-Finish 980). The twenty-third phase meant nothing at the moment, but he had two thoughts about the numbers.

One was about countdowns, as the numbers were reversed, was it a countdown to zero, like the launch of a rocket? The second was the fact he'd realised that 980 was half of 1960. He decided to assume they were years, on the same basis as before, namely the document was in a 'language' he would understand. He thought about it for a while and decided he would explore the idea of a countdown first.

He started by halving the numbers, 1960—980—490— 245—122.5—61.25—30.625. He realised that he was getting into an ever-increasing line of decimal places, he didn't even know if he was on the right track yet? It would get too complex if he went further, the growing number of decimal places would represent fractions of a year—that, he felt would be ridiculous. It could be a totally different kind of time anyway, so at this early stage he'd keep it simple. He decided to round to the nearest whole number, rounding down a point five or below, as he was going down. He then continued with the halving process—245-122-61-31-15-8-4-2-1-0—twelve steps in all. Now to go in the opposite direction, if it was a countdown, where had it started?

1960-3921-7842-15684-31368-62736, etc., etc. He had almost given up doubling as the figure had grown into billions, when, at the twenty-first step he got to 4,110,417,920—and suddenly stopped.

This number prompted a sudden thought, could this be the number of the planet reference? He checked with his photocopy of the document. Yes, it might be possible, although it was only the first four digits. He experienced a slight frisson of excitement at the possibility that he might actually be on the right track?

He continued. The next was 8,220,835,840 and the one after that 16,441,671,680. He became even more excited. He knew that the universe was reckoned to be some sixteen billion years old? He made a complete list, on the computer, of what he now thought of as thirty-five steps of time, from the sixteen billion number down to zero, and ran-off some copies.

The following evening, having reflected at some length on what he had done, Christopher fetched four copies of his steps of time hypothesis. He then said to the rest of the family, "I spent some time yesterday playing with the two numbers,

1960 and 980 on the document, I thought they might be years. I don't know if you noticed, but one is half the other?"

"No," said his mother and sister, almost in unison, "I hadn't noticed."

"I came up with something that might prove to be interesting," he went on to explain what he had done. "I've made a list—here are the copies. I've thought about it a bit since I did it and there are three things that come to mind that are quite interesting.

"As you can see, it starts at 16,445,864,960. I stopped at that point because I thought it might be the age of the universe. Secondly, look at the third number down, 4,110,417,920, it reminded me of the 4.110 planet reference on the document.

"I had wondered if it could be the date when the Earth was created, but that is well established at four point six billion years ago? I've thought about it since and have a possible explanation, but I'll come back to that.

"The third point is potentially the most interesting. If the life of the world were on a countdown, halving the number of years at each step means that zero would of course be the final step! That implies, if this hypothesis is correct, that the life of the world is finite! I'd never thought of the Earth as having a finite lifespan. Like most people I guess I just assumed it would go on for thousands, if not millions of years yet, it's a very salutary thought."

Helen broke the silence that ensued, with a further idea, "If your hypothesis was valid, it would be very relevant to know where we are now, on your steps of time, as you call them?" There was an understandable lull in the conversation, as the implications of what Helen had just said, sunk in.

After a short while, Pat suggested, "Assuming the document's real, and if this ever-shortening timescale is the case, it could help to explain God's concern at the Soul Yield Falling—why there is a sense of urgency in taking action by decree."

The reaction to Christopher's hypothesis contained some very big ifs, and thus provided much food for thought; it had brought a new dimension to the document. Now, for the first time, their speculation had begun to take form.

Eugene asked Christopher, "You said you had thought about the problem of the age of the Earth, the two different figures?"

"I've been rereading that book on astronomy you and mum gave me, particularly the chapter on when and how the Earth was formed. It is thought that the sun was created from a massive explosion, which formed our galaxy about five billion years ago. In addition to the sun, there were a lot of smaller bits of white-hot matter thrown out at the same time. They were not large enough to maintain nuclear fission like the sun, but some of this matter circled our sun and became the building material of Earth and the other planets in our solar system.

"The building process, which formed the Earth and planets, was completed 4.6 billion years ago. By then, let's say, the surface had cooled down from white-hot to red-hot. It continued to cool gradually, but was not sufficiently cool on the surface at least, to enable the Earth to develop any further, until 4,110,417,920 years ago? We all know that the core is still red-hot and molten, even today."

"You certainly have thought about it," said his father. "That's an ingenious way of solving the apparent difference in time, congratulations. It sounds like a credible explanation to me."

He had promised to phone Thea once he had worked on the numbers to report progress, if any. He now wanted to share his thoughts with her, as he had with the family, albeit it was quite late.

"Thea, it's Christopher, how are you?"

"Fine thanks; it's nice of you to phone. Nice timing, I've just finished for the evening."

"Did you have a good journey and how's work going?"

"Yes I did thanks; the Eurostar service to Brussels is excellent. Work's going well, but I've been asked to obtain information on the ten new member states due to join the EU in May 2004. I don't have to visit them, but get what I can here; unfortunately it means I'll have to stay at least an extra week."

"That is a pity, I was looking forward to seeing you at the end of next week. Where are you staying?"

"I'm in a comfortable bed and breakfast hotel called the Mayfair, on the Avenue Louise, going south from the centre of Brussels. It's mainly residential, relatively quiet and near a park called the Bois de la Cambre, where I can go for a stroll. Also, there's a super little restaurant called George V, it's a bit expensive, but a real treat for the occasional evening meal."

"That sounds good. I phoned to tell you how I'd got on with the numbers so far, as you asked."

"Oh good, so tell me."

Christopher then explained what he had done so far, with the galaxy and star references. He also thought he might have resolved the 03 and the 4.110 in the planet reference, but was stuck on the last part. He concluded with his thirty-five steps of time hypothesis.

"Could they be the phases referred to in the document?" Thea asked.

"That's a bright idea Thea, it's possible, I'll give it some thought. Helen suggested that if the steps of time are valid, then we really need to know where the world is now, before we can make further progress, but I can't see how to do that at the moment."

"If your hypothesis is right Chris, and it starts with the creation of the universe, maybe you could see if the early history of the world's evolution fits your steps of time. If it does, you might begin to get some idea of timing."

"That sounds like another really good idea, Thea, thanks. It's not something I know much about, but I'll go down to the library and see what I can find. I've just realised your one hour ahead, it's getting late."

"Don't worry, your calls cheered me up, I don't feel quite so alone, but I think you're right, it's time for bed, thanks again for calling, good night and God bless."

"Good night Thea, I'll phone again soon."

When he woke, he was keen to follow-up Thea's suggestion? He needed to understand the evolution of the world and its flora and fauna. Then he might begin to be able to make sense of the thirty-five steps of time.

He went to the reference section of Maidenhead library to see what he could find. With some initial help from a librarian, he found a number of books on the subject. He spent a good part of the day browsing through each, making notes and photocopying some pages for reference purposes. In the front of one of the last books he found a particularly helpful two-page spread, it was a summary chart, headed 'The Ages of the Earth'.

It laid out the four eras of time: Precambrian, Palaeozoic, Mesozoic and Cenozoic. These Eras were sub-divided into thirteen periods: The Archeozoic through to the Quaternary. The last two periods, the Tertiary and Quaternary, were further sub-divided into a total of seven Epochs. Against these multiple divisions of time was given the timescale for each, in millions of years, from 4.6 billion years ago, almost to the present time. The chart gave brief details of the world's evolving geography, climate, flora and fauna, through each step of this huge time span. Just what he wanted. He finally went home very satisfied with his few hours' research.

When he got home, he studied the chart he'd obtained and was very surprised at how much information it contained. He studied it for the rest of the day, trying to understand it and finally attempting to match his steps of time with the chart; it proved to be impossible. He was disappointed for the Precambrian Era, which started 4,600 million years ago, had little information and the next step, the Cambrian Period didn't start until 570 million years ago, a time gap of 4,030 million years that was virtually empty.

Thinking about this, he realised that unless some proof existed on Earth, which could be found and carbon-dated, nothing could be listed as having happened. Feeling somewhat thwarted, the only other book he could think of was the first book of the bible, Genesis. It started with God's creation of the universe and the world, why not give that a try?

Reading Genesis, within the context of his hypothesis, it had more meaning for him than it ever had before. He thought about it for a while and decided to write out each of God's commands in sequence, in shortened form—creating the universe, creating light, creating night and day, creating sky, clouds, rain and water, land and sea, plants, etc. Suddenly he realised he was well into where the chart began, and so he was now able to resolve his initial difficulty to some extent.

Using his notes and material from the library, he was able to complete the list. The first big surprise was that the sequence of events in Genesis was exactly the same as that which mankind had deduced from all its research! The next thing that came as a surprise was the time it took for each of God's commands to come to fruition; they were not instantaneous as the bible intimated. The third surprise was that each step in the evolutionary process overlapped with one or more of those that followed. When command was issued and the process started to develop, it continued to do so beyond that day of creation into the subsequent day or days, even while further commands were given.

Encouraged though he was, the big snag he faced was that Genesis said it took six days, yet evolution had taken 16 billion years? He wrestled with this problem for some days, looking up facts in his astronomy books and eventually he reached a tentative conclusion.

After all, he'd said to himself, what is a day? —daylight hours? —twenty-four hours? —or just a period of time? If the latter, what period of time? Was one rotation of a 'heavenly' body the criteria, like Earth's day? If so, Jupiter's day is shorter than ours is, just 9hrs 55mins; whereas Mercury's day is 58.6 of our days; Venus's 243.2 of our days. Then, moving to the extreme, one rotation of our galaxy, the Milky Way, takes 225 million years (a cosmic year) but only a day, if measured by the same single rotational criteria.

What is time anyway, he had also asked himself? He was encouraged in his thinking by his emergent understanding of Einstein's theory. He was the first man to realise that time is also a variable dimension. So, Christopher reasoned why should our egotistical nature assume a Genesis Day is Earth's length of day? The inspired scribe of Genesis simply knew of no other time span!

He still had one further snag to overcome if his hypothesis was correct. Each of the steps of time was half the length of the previous step, if these steps were Genesis days, how could the days diminish in length of time? He was pleased with his logic and his conclusions, so far as they went, but a possible solution to this last snag escaped him for the moment. He decided to discuss it all with his father.

His father was impressed by his son's logical approach to the problem and recognised the further problem he faced.

"It reminds me of a book I once read, quite a while ago," he said. "It was by Alvin Toffler, called 'Future Shock'. In it, he talks about the way time seems to be accelerating. I remember one example, he cited the average speed of the old camel trains across the desert, then plotted each further step of increased speed against calendar time, right through to supersonic travel of today. He showed that travelling didn't just get faster, but that both the pace and rate of change also clearly accelerated over the years."

"A kind of logarithmic progression, eh dad? Each step being half the length of the previous step is in fact equidistant when plotted on log-paper. Yeah, I can see it clearly now, each day can be seen as being of the same length; it just depends on how one chooses to look at it."

"Yeah, that's a good analogy Chris. But following that train of thought, why do you think you had to round the decimal places of the shorter steps?"

"I wondered that myself afterwards, dad. I concluded that whoever wrote the document knew exactly the year, the month, the week, the day and the hour that the world will end, but had to translate it into Earthly time. Similarly referring to our words, our short forms, like *Sp* for spiral and *'CC'* for *Carina Centauri* and also our distance measurements with *27K* for 27,000 light years. Thanks dad, it's surprising how a brief chat can clear one's thinking."

Now satisfied that a Genesis day could be of any length and that the length of each subsequent day could be halved, Christopher began to lay out the steps of time, starting at 16.4 billion, then 8.2 billion, 4.1 billion, etc.

He studied his notes from the first chapter of Genesis and almost immediately hit a snag. Sixteen point four billion, God created the universe and the world at four point six billion, there was nothing in Genesis for eight point two billion— absolutely nothing?

He chose to ignore the problem for the moment, to see if the rest worked out. If he started at eight point two instead of sixteen point four billion it would fit. An added reason to temporarily ignore the sixteen billion number was that it was theoretical, no positive proof existed, so far as he knew. Whereas there was positive proof, from rock finds on Earth regarding the date of four point six billion years.

Hypothetically then, Day One commenced eight point two billion years ago. God created the universe, light, night and day, and then the Earth.

Day Two commenced four point one billion years ago. God created a dome called sky and it separated water above from water below.

Day Three commenced two point zero five billion years ago. God created land, which He called earth, and the sea. Then He commanded the earth to produce all kinds of plants.

Day Four commenced one point zero two eight billion years ago. The sun, the moon and the stars appeared in the sky. (Christopher thought that seemed very odd as they already existed? There would have to be an explanation for that anomaly somewhere?)

Day Five commenced five hundred and fourteen million years ago. God created the fish in the sea and the birds in the air.

Day Six commenced two hundred and fifty-seven million years ago. God created the animals and then he said *"we will make human beings."* He paused at this saying to himself, but there is very firm evidence that they only appeared some three point four million years ago? Day six appeared to finish one hundred and twenty-eight and a half million years ago; day six just didn't fit his hypothesis at all?

He felt bitterly disappointed. He had wrestled with the problem, tried to fathom it out, but now it appeared to be a double disaster. The sixteen billion number didn't fit, and now day six didn't fit either? Additionally, what about the sun, moon and stars appearing on day four? It was all very depressing.

When Helen's A-level results came through the post, she screamed with delight after opening the envelope, she had achieved better grades than she needed for her entry to Imperial College. Mum, dad; even Christopher gave her a kiss and a hug of congratulations. She was able to agree a gap year, confirming her place at St Mary's Hospital Medical School. She was also able to confirm her visit to Pattaya.

The family had a celebratory dinner at a local restaurant that evening. Surprisingly it was at that dinner that the next breakthrough regarding the document occurred. They were discussing Christopher's impasse when Helen happened to say, "I wonder Chris, if the 'M' and 'C' in the planet reference could conceivably refer to Mankind's and Christ's appearance on Earth?" The wine, her newfound self-confidence and a sudden insight enabled her to voice this possibility.

They had got to the coffee stage when Pat said to Christopher. "Helen's idea has just prompted another thought. I feel sure that later in Genesis it gives the ages at which each generation was born, from Adam right down to Abraham I think, why don't you take a look at it tomorrow. I'm not sure, but you might be able to calculate how long it was from the time of Adam and Eve, to when Christ was born? You can then see if the number of years fits with any of your steps of time."

Chris was grateful for Helen's idea and his mother's suggestion saying, "Thanks both of you, I'll certainly give it a try."

Christopher turned the pages of Genesis until he came across the first set of generation years that his mother had recalled; they were in chapter five.

Christopher started to make a list of the years. *Adam was 130 years old; he had a son who was like him, and he named him Seth... When Seth was 105, he had a son, Enosh...etc.* Then finally, *After Noah was 500 years old, he had three sons, Shem, Ham and Japeth.* He added up the numbers, they totalled 1,556 years.

He had yet to come to Abraham so he carried on turning pages until he came to chapter eleven. The next set of numbers started at verse ten. *These are the descendants of Shem. Two years after the flood, when Shem was 100 years old, he had a son, Arpachshad...etc.* Until he reached... *After Terah was 70 years old, he became the father of Abram.*

"That's only another 390 years that still only makes the total 1,946 years, there must be more?"

He carried on looking and didn't have far to go—it was on the next page, in chapter twelve. It read *When Abram was seventy-five years old... "This is the country I am going to give to your descendants."* So, Christopher added another 75 years, making the cumulative total 2,021 years. It still didn't seem enough, but in spite of going through the rest of Genesis there was nothing else of relevance, so how to get from Abraham at 75 to Christ?

He went to find his mother and said, "I've been right through Genesis and found the age at which each generation was born up to Abraham, as you suggested, but nothing from there to Christ?"

"Oh, you wouldn't, sorry, I forgot to mention that's not in Genesis, Chris, you'll find it in the back. There's a chart of biblical history, I think you'll find it there?"

"Thanks mum, I'll go take a look."

Returning to the study he soon found the chart. It read, 'Abraham comes to Palestine c.1900 BC.' Christopher added this figure, giving him a grand total of 3,921 years from Adam & Eve to Christ. It was still a much smaller number than he expected, but running his finger down his list of the steps of time, he suddenly shouted, "Eureka, that's it!" It was almost exactly one of the steps of time, from 7840 down to 3920, it's just one year out. If one said 1,899 years in place of 'circa 1,900 BC,' it would be exactly right. Now that's what I call real cool, he thought.

He was so excited, he jumped up, found his mother again and giving her a kiss, said, "You're brilliant, your idea really worked mum, I can now put the steps of time into context. He then went on to explain how the two numbers tallied within a year.

"Be careful when you do it Chris, do you remember, in late '99 as the millennium approached, some of the media made the point it wasn't really 2,000 years since the birth of Christ, in fact it had already passed."

"Now you come to mention it, I do vaguely remember something about it."

"You'll need to check your dates, the actual date is still disputed, but I think you'll find that same biblical chart says Christ was born in 6 BC."

Having thanked his mother once again, he returned to the study and found his mother was right, the footnote to the chart said *the birth of Christ took place about six years BC.* That would mean 3920 in his steps of time was equal to 6 BC, and that 7840, the step back in time, would be the date when God created Adam and Eve!"

If 3920 is 6 BC, (he wrote this date in pencil alongside that number on his steps of time copy). Then that makes 7840 on my scale equal to 3,926 BC in our time, and going forward, 1960 becomes 1954 AD. (He wrote in these new dates in pencil also).

Pondering this exciting conclusion, he called to mind the planet reference M21C. If 'M' did represent the first of mankind, in the form of Adam and Eve, and 'C' the birth of Christ, then 21 could be the twenty-first step of time or the twenty-first phase? Excitedly he counted the number of steps from the sixteen billion number, but his hopes were dashed when he found it was step twenty-two? If he continued to ignore the sixteen billion number, and started at the eight billion number, it would then be step twenty-one.

There must be an explanation, he thought, that's the second time I need to ignore the sixteen billion number to make things fit? But setting that aside for the moment, he realised there was another problem. Hominids, the first identifiable human, appeared about three point four million years ago and 3,926 BC for Adam and Eve is nowhere near it! Throwing his pencil down he said to himself, each time I appear to be making progress I come to yet another seemingly intractable problem!

At their evening meal Christopher was a bit subdued. He told them how well his mother's idea had worked out, but went on to explain how it presented yet another seemingly intractable problem.

Helen asked, "Now you've established that 1960 on your steps of time, is probably 1954 in our time, when does the world get to zero?"

"It's a countdown, Helen, so in 1954 there were still one thousand, nine hundred and sixty years to go; adding that on means it will be 3914, so year zero will be AD 3915.

"I feel a bit jaded at the moment, it seems to be two steps forward and one back, and I need a break. I think I'll phone Thea, a weekend in Brussels would be a good break. She told me she's got to stay at least an extra week, so I'll suggest I go over for the coming weekend."

"That's a good idea," said his mother, "but you need to take a proper holiday before you go back to Cambridge, a weekend's not enough."

"I'll think about it, mum, but you know how I get bored if I have nothing much to do, this document is a good challenge, even if it is a bit frustrating." He phoned Thea after dinner, she was delighted at the idea, and was easily able to book him into the Mayfair from Friday to Sunday night, at a weekend rate, as it was essentially a weekday business hotel.

Chapter Three
Conviction

Christopher caught the 3:00 pm Eurostar on Friday afternoon, arriving at Brussels Midi station just on 6:30pm local time. Thea met him, and although this was only the third time they'd met, they greeted each other like old friends with a much less self-conscious hug and a kiss.

Thea had told the hotel he would be late arriving, and suggested they take a taxi to the Grand Place. They spent some time admiring the picturesque buildings round the square, and then found a small restaurant in one of the side streets off the square, for a leisurely evening meal.

Their conversation covered Thea's initial thoughts about Brussels and comparisons to what she had seen of other European capitals so far. She also mentioned she'd booked them on a sightseeing tour for a good part of Saturday. They each talked more about their families, but inevitably they returned to the document.

Thea said, "Thinking about the document address as you called it, don't you think it implies there are many more worlds with life on them, not just ours?"

"Yeah, I agree, I don't know if it will ever be proven though. To think that we are the only beings in the universe is probably too egotistical, a bit like the Catholic church excommunicating Copernicus when he had the audacity to suggest that the Earth revolved about the sun, although they did subsequently apologise."

"But scientists are looking for signs of life in the universe aren't they Chris?" "I'm sure they'll find simple life forms, microbes or higher orders, that haven't had the chance to develop, but I doubt they will ever come across advanced civilisations. They're mainly relying on picking up meaningful radio signals, but I think there are two reasons why they probably won't succeed. The distances in space are so vast that I think any transmissions, if they are at our puny power level, would be attenuated to the point of being indistinguishable from any background noise. Secondly, we've had radio for just over a hundred years, we could have it for over two thousand, if we've got 1,960 years to go, but that's still only one ten-millionth of the age of the universe. Worlds have probably formed and died before us and the process will no doubt continue after us. But for two civilisations, on two planets, to be at similar stages of radio development at the same time, and close enough to hear each other, would be an almost unbelievable coincidence."

"Chris, I didn't understand when you tried to explained over the phone, how the length of each step of time was half the one before, yet each could possibly be a Genesis day?"

"Dad and I got into logarithms to sort it out in our minds; it all depends how one chooses to look at it. I think the way the speed of travel has changed will show what I meant. Ages ago we walked or ran, then went by camel or horse, then by bike, car, tram or train. After that came air travel, and finally space rockets.

"Imagine each step of progress enabled travellers to move twice as fast as before, they could then cover the same distance in half the time. So, if we measure each step by distance covered, and not by time, they would all be the same. If the steps of time idea is right, then that's how the Earth has progressed. It has built on what has gone before, enabling it to make a similar amount of progress in half the time, at each step along the way.

"Additionally, our idea of a day is fixed, determined by the Earth's rotation, whereas any day in the universe, in the final analysis, is simply a period of time, measured by whatever yardstick one might choose."

"I think I begin to grasp the idea and see what you mean."

Christopher then brought Thea up to date on the research he had done in the library. How early history, with the help of the bible, had worked out well for days one to five, but only if he ignored the sixteen billion number. But then it broke down completely on day six. This led him on to explain Helen's idea of mankind and Christ from the M21C. Then his mother's idea of timing from the bible, how long it was from Adam & Eve to Christ.

Excitingly it fitted with step twenty-two or twenty-one if he again ignored the sixteen billion number. With two pressure points, it was emerging as a major issue to be resolved. In a way it was even worse because it did not correlate with the known date of the appearance of humankind on Earth.

They agreed the document was presenting some very difficult problems, but were both fascinated and encouraged at how some elements of the jigsaw had begun to clarify.

Their belief in the veracity of the document was growing, but fitting all the pieces together was going to be a real challenge.

Having enjoyed the meal, they went for a little stroll and then took a taxi back to the hotel. After Chris checked-in they took the lift to the second floor and had a slightly lingering hug and kiss when Thea thanked him for a pleasant evening and a lovely meal. They agreed to meet for breakfast at 8.00am and went to their rooms.

At breakfast next morning Thea said, "My parents gave me a beautiful bible when I was confirmed—I take it with me whenever I travel. You remember last night we were talking about days one to six and your use of the bible. Well, I think I might have found a clue to the human timing problem on day six. I decided to reread the first part of Genesis again last night, I noticed something interesting, there's a significant difference when it comes to day six. Up to day five it says *'God commanded'* this or that, but on day six it says, *Then God said, "And now we will make human beings."* It's not a direct command, it implies it will take longer; come to fruition at a later date.

"I didn't notice that, it just didn't register at all, Thea, you're not just clever, you're brilliant. Can I take a look when we get back; it might give me the latitude I need towards solving the timing problem. You seem to have the knack of coming up with clues to progress; that's the second time you've broken a potential logjam."

They went on the sightseeing tour. They were very impressed with the history of the Grand Place as told by their guide; they had a laugh over the Manneken Pis, and saw the old Atomium and the headquarters building of the European Commission, among other things. They were also impressed by the many underpasses at crossroads, which undoubtedly eased traffic congestion. During the tour there was a half-hour-shopping period, Christopher bought his mother some nice Brussels lace place settings in emerald green linen and small gifts for his father and Helen.

When the tour ended, they took a taxi back to the hotel. At Thea's suggestion they went to her room. She made tea while he reread the first part of Genesis, enabling him to understand more fully the context of her breakfast suggestion.

After they'd freshened up, and as they strolled along to the George V restaurant for dinner, Chris was somewhat preoccupied. They selected a Chateaubriand, a Beaune and Parma ham, with melon to start. The waiter pointed out that there would be a delay of at least thirty minutes for the steak; they didn't mind they had the whole evening.

Once they'd ordered Chris explained his preoccupation. "From the research I did, I can see how your idea could cover the period up to the time humankind appeared. But I can't see how it can also cover the period until Adam and Eve appeared? There has to be some other explanation for that."

"I see what you mean; humankind appeared over three million years before Adam and Eve, if both the anthropologists and the biblical timing are to be believed."

Anyway, let's enjoy the meal. I'll work on it when I get back. The way things are going I'm pretty sure an explanation will emerge eventually.

At that moment the steaks arrived. They were surprised to see they had been cooked in paper bags, which were singed brown. The waiter explained it sealed-in all the flavour. It proved to be the best steak they had ever had, tasty and succulent, quite beautiful.

Over dessert and coffee, they were relaxed in each other's company. They lapsed into companionable silences from time to time, each with their own thoughts. Being young their thoughts not only ranged between what they thought of each other and the quest that was the document, but also sex.

He thought how beautiful she was and how well she'd dressed for the evening. How much he wanted her and wanted to be with her. He knew he was beginning to fall in love. He had once indulged in recreational sex, but the downside had taught him that it would only feel really right inside a marriage. He didn't want to jeopardise this burgeoning relationship.

Thea felt very comfortable in Chris' company, he felt more and more like the man she had been waiting for. From what she now knew, their meeting at Stonehenge seemed like random chance, but when added to the discovery of the document, the religious context, and how she felt about him, she was virtually convinced.

She was still a virgin, having resolved long ago that she wanted her husband to know that he was the first man in her life. But nonetheless she decided to play with fire and invite him to her room, a test, to see if he would accept. She instinctively knew that if he refused the temptation, she would be certain he was the man for whom she had been waiting.

They strolled back to the hotel, hand-in-hand, took the lift to their floor and kissed each other a very tender good night. She felt his tumescence as they embraced and said, "Would you like to come to my room Chris?" He graciously declined, saying, "Yes I would love to Thea, but I respect who you are and I don't want to sully our relationship, I hope you're not offended."

"Not at all, Chris, I just wanted you to know I feel the same way as you, we will know when the right moment comes." With that mutual understanding, they embraced once more and then reluctantly went to their rooms, she now convinced, he wondering at his self-restraint.

On Sunday morning, Christopher decided to accompany Thea to mass at a local Catholic church. In spite of it being in French, he was surprised at how similar mass was to the Sunday Service at his local Anglican Church. During the service he recalled his promise to reflect more deeply on his vision—the extraordinary precursor of this rather unusual summer holiday.

Christopher reached a decision; he would share his vision with Thea. He felt increasingly sure that she had a key part to play in solving the meaning of the document. He trusted her to understand and not laugh at his suggestion that he had seen a vision.

After church they decided to walk to the park, the Bois de la Cambre. They compared notes on the similarity between the Catholic and Anglican services. Thea then spoke about how fate seemed to have brought them together at Stonehenge and how the document had drawn them closer.

Chris agreed, then confided in her as to what had happened just before they met. As he told her the details, she became more and more excited. When he'd finished, she said, "It's extraordinary, the evening I got the translation from my father, I decided to read Revelation. I wanted to see if there was anything in there about the future that related in any way to the contents of the document. I didn't find anything, but I'm sure I read about your vision. Let's go back and see if we can find it."

They hurried back to the hotel and up to her room. After a short while she found what she was looking for and handed it to him. He was absolutely flabbergasted when he read. *At once the spirit took control of me. There in heaven was a throne with someone sitting on it. His face gleamed like such precious stones as jasper and carnelian, and all round the throne there was a rainbow the colour of an emerald.*

He went quite pale, humbled to fully comprehend at last, that he really had seen a vision. He was reluctant to admit it to himself. Why me he thought, I'm not holy, I'm not even very spiritual, in fact I was losing interest in religion. But prompted by the memory of his mother's teaching, years ago, and the latter part of his dream, he said to Thea, "Could we see if there is a passage in the bible where God banishes Satan?"

She said she couldn't recall where it might be, so turned to the index at the back. She showed him, there was a list of forty references under Beelzebub, the Devil and Satan. While she read them out, he wrote them down, then they began to work their way through them.

By the time they got to number twenty-six they were beginning to wonder if and when they might find it, but turning to the twenty-seventh reference there it was. In St Luke's gospel they read, *Jesus answered them, "I saw Satan fall like lightening from heaven."* In spite of hoping to find something more, he was dumbfounded—it was a very succinct statement of exactly what he had seen!

Christopher explained to Thea that he was now convinced the events at Stonehenge were linked and had a purpose. The vision, the document, and meeting Thea, were a trinity of events, so close together, they were as one. He now felt he was being led along a path, he was even keener to follow, in spite of having no idea where it led.

Thea in turn told him that from a young age, she couldn't remember when, she would meet and help a man given a special mission in life. She was now convinced, that here it was—he was that man.

It was by now, well into the afternoon, but having eaten well for the last two evenings, they were still not very hungry. They decided to take a taxi into the centre of the city and find a restaurant for an early evening meal.

During the meal they were very happy in each other's company, now knowing they shared a common purpose. They knew the first step was to solve the conundrum of the document, after that, who knows.

Suddenly Thea said "Dad's all alone and really missing me. I've got two weeks holiday to come, so I've said I'd go home for a couple of weeks. I'm sorry to spring it on you, but why don't you come over, you said your mother wanted you to take a proper holiday? Dad said he will take his holiday at the same time as me, so I'm going when I've finished here. I've kept him up to date on progress, because he's still intrigued by the document, he's even said how much he'd like to meet you. We'd love to show you something of Boston, a feel for America. You can tell him first-hand how you're getting on. You can have the spare bedroom, I'm sure he'd be more than pleased, if you agreed to come.

"Do you make a habit of jumping good ideas on people Thea?" He said with a laugh. "That would be wonderful, I'd love to see something of America, you're sure your father wouldn't mind?"

"I know he'd be delighted."

On the way back to the hotel, Thea reflected on the fact that she was falling in love. She somehow knew he was destined to be her husband, and she was destined to play a key-supporting role in her husband's life. She was so pleased that Chris was that man. She knew he was destined for great things, the one who would change the way the world sees itself—the way the world thinks.

Back at the hotel, by agreement, they had an early night. She had to work next day and he would catch an early train home. They kissed each other rather like brother and sister, a tacit understanding after last night's lustful embrace, it was not to be part of their current life.

In the taxi next morning they decided to swap email addresses to make keeping in touch even easier. They said their fond farewells as Thea got out to go to work, then Chris carried on to Midi station to catch his train.

Christopher had a two and a half-hour journey back to Waterloo. As he settled down and began thinking back over the last two or three weeks, and the last two days in particular. He realised he was at the epicentre of this perplexing whirlpool of events, drawing him further and further in, but to what end? He felt his life was being orchestrated, he had to discover why? Thea was undoubtedly a catalyst to the events that were suddenly surrounding his life. Her suggestion about God's commands was clearly a contribution to his investigation? But where did the vision fit in? His mind was in turmoil.

He noticed the despondency of last week had left him, he was keen to try and resolve the document's agenda once more. First, he began to think about what he'd read on the evolution of fauna, how it might be possible to take Thea's point about *'will make'* human beings. Slowly a possible solution began to emerge.

He then turned to the equally, if not more important issue, of having twenty-two steps of time where twenty-one seemed to be called for? The document pointed to the eight billion-year solution that he had so glibly assumed. How could he reconcile such a massive discrepancy? He spent the remaining time wrestling with this huge question. By the time he reached Waterloo he could envisage one potential solution. He had remembered a BBC 2 space programme, a couple of years ago. A man named something like Macuso had suggested that the speed of light was not an absolute, as Einstein had stated. He would have to think much more deeply on the matter and see if this germ of an idea could lead to a solution?

Chapter Four
Status

Christopher phoned home on his mobile, once he was on his way. He told his mother he'd be home in time for lunch as the hour difference was now in his favour.

Over lunch he told his family what a nice break it had been. He'd got on well with Thea who was now a firm friend. He also mentioned he was thinking of going to Boston in a couple of weeks, for a proper holiday, to stay with Thea and her father, probably for a week or so.

After lunch, his mother told him that while he'd been away, she'd finally got round to answering his request. She'd chosen four biblical extracts to answer his question about the 'Current Status' items in the document. She handed him a piece of paper, saying "there are two references for each of the two points—Satan Licensed and Soul Yield Falling."

"Thanks mum, I'll go and look them up."

Looking at the piece of paper, the first item read: Satan Licensed:

- Old Testament—Job 1:1- 2:10. Prologue

- New Testament—Luke 22:31

So, he read: *"There was a man named Job, living in the land of Uz…"* and it went on to explain he was the richest man in the east. He had seven sons, three daughters and literally thousands of sheep, camels, cattle and donkeys. By this stage, recalling his vision, Christopher felt as if he was there, could hear the voices and became deeply immersed in the story.

When the day came for the heavenly beings to appear before the Lord, Satan was there among them. The Lord asked him, "What have you been doing?"

Satan answered; "I have been walking here and there, roaming round the earth."

"Did you notice my servant Job?" The Lord asked. "There is no one on earth as faithful and good as he is. He worships me and is careful not to do anything evil."

Satan replied, "Would Job worship you if he got nothing out of it? You have always protected him and his family and everything he owns. You bless everything he does, and you have given him enough cattle to fill the whole country. But now suppose you take away everything he has—he will curse you to your face!"

"All right," the Lord said to Satan, "everything he has is in your power, but you must not hurt Job himself." So Satan left.

Job lost his seven sons and three daughters, all his sheep, camels, cattle and donkeys, and then a storm swept in from the desert and wrecked his house as well, killing all his servants, bar one.

Then Job stood up and tore his clothes in grief. He shaved his head and threw himself face downwards on the ground. He said, "I was born with nothing, and I will die with nothing.

The Lord gave, and now he has taken away. May his name be praised!"

When the day came for the heavenly beings to appear before the Lord again, Satan was there among them. The Lord asked him, "Where have you been?"

Satan answered; "I have been walking here and there, roaming round the earth."

"Did you notice my servant Job?" the Lord asked. There is no one on earth as faithful and good as he is. He worships me and is careful not to do anything evil. You persuaded me to let you attack him for no reason at all, but Job is still as faithful as ever."

Satan replied, "A man will give up everything in order to stay alive. But now you suppose you hurt his body—he will curse you to your face!"

So, the Lord said to Satan, "All right, he is in your power, but you are not to kill him."

Then Satan left the Lord's presence and made sores break out all over Job's body. Job went and sat by the rubbish heap and took a piece of broken pottery to scrape his sores. His wife said to him, "You are still as faithful as ever, aren't you? Why don't you curse God and die?"

Job answered, "You are talking nonsense! When God sends us something good, we welcome it. How can we complain when he sends us trouble?" In spite of everything he suffered, Job said nothing against God.

Christopher realised from this account that God allowed Satan to roam the earth and tempt people away from worshipping Him. He then turned to the second reference:

"Simon, Simon! Listen! Satan has received permission to test all of you, to separate the good from the bad, as a farmer separates the wheat from the chaff."

Some words spoken in his vision sprang to mind. *"I will replace the fallen angels with new loyal beings who will not rebel—they will have earned their place with me. Those that do not will forever join the rebels without ever setting foot in my kingdom."*

These two passages gave Christopher a much clearer understanding of what 'Satan licensed' meant. He then referred to the second part of his mother's note—both were in the Old Testament—Soul Yield Falling:

- Deuteronomy—8: 12-14.

- Proverbs—30: 7-9.

So he read once more: *When you have all you want to eat and have built good houses to live in and when your cattle and sheep, your silver and gold, and all your other possessions have increased, make sure that you do not become proud and forget the Lord...*

And in Proverbs: *I ask you, God...let me be neither rich nor poor. So give me only as much food as I need. If I have more, I might say that I do not need you. But if I am poor, I might steal and bring disgrace on my God.*

He recognised that the Western World was guilty of the points being made. Belief in God and religious practice had declined. There was a decline in moral standards and a drop in the standard of behaviour that accompanied it. He reflected on his own behaviour, his reduced interest in religion over the last year or so, but that events, and Thea, had given him a renewed spiritual awareness.

The following day, after breakfast, Helen went off to visit friends before going to Thailand, and dad went to his study to catch up on paperwork. Christopher was a little troubled by what he had read the previous afternoon so took the opportunity to talk to his mother as they were now alone.

They were close; he loved her dearly; she not only loved him, but was also proud of him, his looks, his personality and his academic ability. He thanked her for finding the biblical examples, which he'd now read; saying also how the document was taking him into areas of thought he'd never considered before. The study of flora and fauna, for example, was a complete change from math and physics. He was now convinced the document was genuine, so he was keen to understand it's meaning, in depth.

He went on to say, "For example, the treatment of Job made me think of all the problems mankind has to face, not just illness, but natural disasters from floods, landslides, volcanoes and famines. There were also man-made problems such as murders, terrorism and wars. How can a loving God allow mankind to suffer in these ways, has anyone come up with a rationale or a satisfactory explanation?"

"Well, Christopher, it's not easy to explain. When I was at university, we discussed this same question with one of our lecturers at some length. He directed us to the works of Charles Kingsley, which he wrote in the mid to late 1800s. He was rector of a parish in Hampshire, as well as a highly educated and brilliant social novelist. His ideas are the best explanation I've come across, although a bit abstruse, I'll try to summarise.

"Kingsley said God could have chosen to produce a perfect world. But He produced something cleverer, an evolving universe, by bringing into being a creation in which stars, planets and creatures could *make themselves.* This kind of world is good, because it presents people with the opportunity to earn a place with God in heaven, but it has a necessary cost.

"Death is an inevitable part of this evolving universe, be they stars, planets or people, each generation has to give way to the next. Genetic mutations are necessary to generate new forms of life, but they can also cause malignancy, so such things can range from good to bad.

"This kind of creation also allows terrible events to happen. Not because God is callous or incompetent, but because a creation in which stars, planets and creatures make themselves, is necessarily a world of change, ragged edges, blind alleys, a world of transience and death. It causes us to reflect, to recognise the power of God and it offers us a challenge, the opportunity to help one another.

"This world is not the final expression of God's intentions. God's ultimate purpose is that people should be free to choose to enter into, and embrace a life with God. This second step, to enter another form of life with God, after death, is God's final purpose. God showed us how this can happen through Christ's life, death and resurrection."

Some of the words his mother used resonated very strongly with the words he'd heard God speak in his vision. Christopher still felt he couldn't tell his mother about the vision, but now knew its purpose—it had exposed him to the moment He decided to create the universe. He laughed, saying, "Gosh mum, that sounded like a practiced speech, is it something you regularly tell the R.E. girls in the upper sixth?"

His mother laughed as well. "No," she said, "it just happened to come out like that. Kingsley went on to say that we could learn about God from the nature of this creation, that He is not a God in a hurry. God is patient, waiting twelve billion years for any form of life to appear, and a further four billion years for the arrival of self-conscious beings."

"Thanks a lot, mum, Kingsley must have been an interesting character; you've really helped me begin to understand why the world is the way it is. Now I know why you're such a good teacher, although I knew that anyway."

They had forgotten their coffee, lost in his mother's explanation it had gone cold, so Christopher offered to make some more. When he came back with fresh coffee, he said, "While you're into explanations, can you clarify something else for me—is there a story like that one of Job, which illustrates a difference between the behaviour of those that go to heaven and those that go to hell?"

"Oh, that's easy, Chris," she said. "The Parable of the Rich man and Lazarus is probably the best known example, you'll find it in Luke, chapter sixteen, I think."

They then went on to discuss Helen's forthcoming trip to Thailand and Pattaya, as well as his proposed visit to Boston. His mother said "you've only seen Thea three or four times, yet you've stayed three nights in Brussels with her, and now you want to go to Boston. It's getting a bit too involved rather quickly, isn't it, Chris?"

"Yes, I suppose it does seem like that, mum, but don't worry, it's a summer holiday friendship, it's platonic, not a romance. I like her, in fact I like her a lot, I think the feeling's mutual, but the document's the centre of the relationship, not lust or love. She's older than I am, she knows I'm at university, with two years to go, and she'll be back in Boston from the end of this year. To think further than that would be pure speculation."

His mother sensed he was, perhaps, not being totally honest with her or himself, and said, "You'd tell me if your feelings for Thea change wouldn't you Chris?"

"Yes mum, I would."

"When you fix the dates of your visit, assuming Thea's travelling at the weekends, can I suggest you go mid-week to mid-week? That'll give Thea and her father some time to themselves at the beginning and the end of their holiday.

"That's a thoughtful idea mum, I'll do that, thanks."

"Another thing, I think you should invite her here before you go back to Cambridge, give your father and I an opportunity to meet her."

"That's a good suggestion, I'll happily do that. Perhaps she could stay for the weekend, using Helen's room, after she's gone?"

Later that day, Christopher got the bible and found the parable his mother had suggested at verse 19 of chapter sixteen:

There was a rich man who used to dress in purple and fine linen and feast magnificently every day. And at his gate there used to lie a poor man called Lazarus, covered with sores, who longed to fill himself with what fell from the rich man's table. Even dogs came and licked his sores. Now it happened that the poor man died and was carried away by the angels into Abraham's embrace. The rich man also died and was buried.

In his torment in Hades he looked up and saw Abraham a long way off with Lazarus in his embrace. So he cried out, "Father Abraham, pity me and send Lazarus to dip the tip of his finger in water and cool my tongue, for I am in agony in these flames." Abraham said, "My son, remember that during your life you had your fill of good things, just as Lazarus his fill of bad. Now he is being comforted here while you are in agony. But that is not all: between us and you a great gulf has been fixed, to prevent those who want to cross from our side to yours or from your side to ours."

And Christopher again recalled similar words from his vision; "I will create a great gulf between us, so deep and so wide, that you will never be able to return." He read on.

So he said, "Father I beg you then to send Lazarus to my father's house, since I have five brothers, to give them warning so they do not come to this place of torment too." Abraham said, "They have Moses and the prophets, let them listen to them." The rich man replied, "Ah no, father Abraham, but if someone comes to them from the dead, they will repent." Then Abraham said to him, "If they will not listen either to Moses or to the prophets, they will not be convinced even if someone should rise from the dead."
Luke16:27-31

Christopher realised from reading this that Christ was also part of God's plan of creation. He would send Him when mankind had advanced—a time when a permanent record became possible for all the generations to come. He needed to show mankind the way, but not everyone would believe in Him, or his resurrection from the dead-on Easter Sunday.

Chapter Five
Frustration

Christopher had visited the library once again, to gather more information about the evolution of man, to address the suggestion made by Thea...*we will make human beings,* it was undoubtedly a key part of the overall solution.

Looking back at his previous work, Christopher saw that he had to go back about three and a half billion years, into the Precambrian Era, to trace the building blocks from which life was created. Stromatolites were a blue/green mass, consisting of dense mounds of microbes. From there evolved Eukaryotes, about one point five billion years ago. These were an organised cell nucleus surrounded by a membrane. Then emerged Protists, some eight hundred million years ago, containing a contribution from early plant life towards the formation of animal-life DNA, which would be used later.

In the Cambrian Period, about five hundred and seventy million years ago, Graptolites, a form of marine organism emerged. From these came sponges, followed by a range of evolving molluscs, gastropods, nautiloids and trilobites.

He realised what a huge time span he still had to cover, from here to Adam and Eve! It was rather daunting, but he would try to see if he could slowly piece it all together with the help of the photocopy charts, he'd made in the library

Reading through the early part of Genesis once again, he established that the appearance of 'real life' on Earth was at the beginning of day five. It started with God's command, *"Let the water be filled with many kinds of living beings, and let the air be filled with many kinds of birds."*

Day five of creation was on the cusp of the Cambrian/Ordovician periods, almost five hundred and fourteen million years ago. Following God's command, a tremendous adaptive radiation came upon the Earth. From this a wide range of genetic mutations emerged, new groups of Ammonites, Gastropods, Polyzoa—the first sea urchins, all five living orders of starfish and the first vertebrates in the form of jawless fishes.

There was a mass extinction at the end of the Ordovician Period, around four hundred and forty million years ago. This culling lead into the Silurian period, within which a diversification of marine life ensued—the first true jawed fishes, the earliest shark-like fish, sea scorpions and the first bony fishes, evolved.

Starting about four hundred and ten million years ago, in the Devonian Period, the bony fishes themselves diversified. The first land animals appeared about three hundred and sixty million years ago. A photocopied page explained how a four-legged, five-toed fossil, found in Scotland in 1971, had filled what was called Romer's Gap, it illustrated how species of fish began to adapt to the land.

Scorpions and wingless insects appeared around this time. A further selective culling of marine life came at the end of the Devonian Period, about three hundred and fifty-five million years ago.

In this way he slowly worked on through the Carboniferous, Permian, Triassic, Jurassic and Cretaceous periods. Animal life progressed as the periods changed, flying insects to reptiles, mammals, dinosaurs and birds. In the sea there evolved enormous marine reptiles such as Ichthyosaurus, which lived about one hundred and eighty million years ago. Plesiosaurs and Teleosts, which were destined to become the dominant fish group of today.

Finally, Tarsiers, the first of the primates, appeared about sixty-five million years ago, in the Palaeocene Epoch. Christopher followed their development, step by step. Tarsiers to Loris, to Pottos, Bush Babies, Ring Tailed Lemurs and so on through the twenty-seven evolutionary steps, ending with Orangutans, Chimpanzees, and Gorillas, until he got to Hominids, the first of the human beings that lived about three point four million years ago.

Christopher had worked assiduously for most of the day and decided he needed a break. He checked his computer for emails, and was delighted to discover one from Mr Theurgy in Boston. It read:

'Thea told me you'd spent the weekend in Brussels and she'd issued an invitation for you to visit Boston. I was delighted; I'm sure we'll have a great time showing you some of the sights. You're most welcome to stay with us. I suggest you fix the dates with Thea.

'Please bring the original document with you, I'd love to see it, no doubt you can fill me in with your intriguing investigations. I look forward to meeting you, best wishes— Emmanuel Theurgy.'

Christopher ran-off a copy and took it to show his parents, thrilled at the prospect of his first visit to America being so enthusiastically confirmed. "I'll phone Thea this evening to finalise the dates." As he said that he realised that Thea's father was also a Theurgy. He'd already played a vital role with organising the translation, was he yet another influential factor in the mix?

His mother had been reading her copy of 'The Tablet', a weekly magazine which kept her up to date on religious affairs. Passing it to him she said, "Christopher, you remember a couple of weeks ago we talked about the three wise men from the east, guided by a star at the birth of Christ. Well, there's an article in there about the associated astronomy that you'll probably find very interesting."

"Thanks mum," he said, found the article and started reading, soon becoming totally absorbed. When he'd finished, he added, "That's fantastic, what a timely coincidence! Do you mind if I keep it?"

"Not at all, it's yours, I've finished with it."

"Thanks again, mum."

"Hello Thea, it's Chris, how are things?"

"Hi Chris, a bit tedious this evening, I'm emailing sheet after sheet of statistics. I was going to phone you when I'd finished, to cheer myself up a bit, but you've done it for me. Did you get dad's email?"

"Yes, that's mainly why I called. I guessed you'd given him my email address. I was pleasantly surprised how enthusiastic he seemed at the idea of my going over."

"I'm not surprised, he's never ever seen or heard of anything like the document, he's mad keen to talk to you about it." With a smile in her voice she added, "I've also told him you're quite a pleasant young man as well."

"Flatterer! So, have you agreed with your father, when you're going home?"

"Yes, the first two weeks of August. I'm sure to be finished here by then, and it allows me a little time back in Hammersmith to get everything in order. I'm planning to fly to Boston on the Saturday."

"You'll want some time with your father, you've been away for over six months. How about I come over on the following Wednesday for a week?"

"That's very thoughtful Chris, it sounds good to me."

"Right, I'll book my flights tomorrow and let you know the details. I'm getting quite excited at the prospect already."

"Yes, it should be fun. By the way you didn't phone me when you got back home Sunday evening, how'd you like Brussels?"

"Sorry Thea, that was rather thoughtless of me, it was nice seeing you again, I enjoyed the break. The sights were quite good; mum was thrilled with the lace. Apart from seeing you, I thought the best bits were the Grand Place and the meal at the George V."

"Yes I agree—that was a really lovely evening."

"Changing the subject; do you remember I told you about establishing the timescale of the steps of time by when Christ was born?"

"Yes."

"Well, mum came across a super article about the associated astronomy. It fixes the date absolutely; I'll email it to you tomorrow.

"I hope I'll understand it, I'll send it on to dad, he'll be interested."

"I know, I'll do a short write-up for you, instead of sending the article; it is a bit on the long side anyway."

"That sounds better already, I'll look forward to it."

"Well, I guess I'd better let you get back to work and finish your reporting."

"Good bye for now then Chris, God bless."

Dear Thea,

As promised, the main points of the article for you. To make it more interesting, with mum's help, I decided to combine the key points in the article with the biblical text. Mum suggested an extract from Isaiah and the text from St Mathew's gospel, so here goes…

The Three Wise Men

Isaiah, when prophesying the birth of Christ, said:

"But on you the light of the Lord will shine; the brightness of his presence will be with you. Nations will be drawn to your light, and kings to the dawning of your new day.

"Great caravans of camels will come, from Midian and Ephah; they will come from Sheba, bringing gold and incense!"

Mankind, in many parts of the world, had become aware of, and studied the apparent movement of the stars. In Babylon, these movements were used to time the first calendar c.530 BC. Other peoples associated the movement of stars as signs and portents of worldly events to come.

One such portent was the heliacal rising of a star (that is, when it rises and becomes visible at dawn, just before the full light of sunrise 'drowns it out'). In astrological terms the three wise men believed it heralded the birth of a great king. They observed such an event in the east, in a constellation they associated with Judea. So, set out to pay homage and take gifts to the king.

Jesus was born in the town of Bethlehem in Judea, during the time when Herod was king. Soon afterwards, some men who studied the stars came from the east to Jerusalem and asked, "Where is the baby born to be the king of the Jews? We saw his star when it came up in the east, and we have come to worship him." But nobody knew.

Now comes one of the most interesting bits. As they came into Jerusalem the star disappeared, (the moon was passing in front of it—an occultation) so they went to King Herod, thinking it would be his progeny; but of course, it was not.

When King Herod heard about this, he was very upset, and so was everyone else in Jerusalem. He called together all the chief priests and the teachers of the law and asked them, "Where will the Messiah be born?"

"In the town of Bethlehem in Judea," they answered, for this is what the prophet wrote:

'Bethlehem in the land of Judah, you are by no means the least of the leading cities of Judah; for from you will come a leader who will guide my people Israel.'

So Herod called the visitors from the east to a secret meeting and…he sent them to Bethlehem…

The Magi then left Herod, and approached Bethlehem from the west. The time span of occultation of the star behind the moon (it was in fact Jupiter, which at that time was thought to be a star) had now passed.

And so they left, and on their way they saw the same star they had seen in the east. When they saw it, how happy they were, what joy was theirs!
It went ahead of them until it stopped over the place where the child was.

Now comes the tricky bit about relative motion (a bit like the effect of two trains, side-by-side, moving at slightly different speeds in a station). The Earth, moving faster in its orbit around the sun than Jupiter, was overtaking it, and it was this that created an optical illusion as a result of their relative motion. The alignment of the two planets caused Jupiter to appear to become stationary against the background of stars, for a short period, as the Earth moved that bit faster than Jupiter. A computer backwardation shows that this sequence of events actually took place; Jupiter appeared to stand still on the 17th of April, 6 BC!

"They went into the house, and when they saw the child with his mother Mary, they knelt down and worshipped him. They brought their gifts of gold, frankincense, and myrrh, and presented them to him."

So, the debate about the year of Christ's birth is finally put to rest. It prompted me to have another thought, not relevant to the document, but potentially interesting nonetheless. When I go back to Cambridge, I'll try to get someone to see if a backwardation of eclipses of the sun can be run? If it can, I'll see if one took place in Israel on a Friday afternoon, let's say sometime between AD 25 and 30, to account for the darkness talked about in the gospels at Christ's crucifixion.

Of course, it might not have been an eclipse, but just a very heavy overcast. In case that is the explanation, could you ask your father to enquire if anyone who's heavily into Roman literature, has ever found a reference to earthquakes or tremors, around those dates, in Israel? If you recall the veil of the temple was torn in two. It would be even more fantastic if an eclipse and an earth tremor came together, sometime between those two years, that would also fix the date of Christ's crucifixion.

Having sent the email, Christopher returned to the task he'd left the day before. He set about trying to meld his list of the evolution of the species, into the steps of time.

He traced evolution, slowly and methodically, down through ten steps of time. From step two or three to twelve or thirteen, when human beings were first known to have appeared in the form of Hominids, around three point four million years ago. This again highlighted the unresolved problem—the initial date of the universe's creation.

There were at least eight or nine major world events (he wasn't sure if two were in fact one that lasted a much longer time that the others). They played a significant part in shaping the course of evolution. Four were caused by adaptive radiation, which lead to genetic mutations that changed the direction of the evolutionary process. The other four or five were cataclysmic physical events. So he spent time reviewing what informed opinion had to say of them all.

He turned first to the four periods of adaptive radiation; it was thought they were probably due to the earth being bombarded with intense radiation from the explosion of super novae.

The others were put down to a variety of possibilities—at least two were attributed to huge comet or asteroid impacts. The first of these was around two hundred and fifty million years ago, which was on the cusp of steps six and seven of time. It produced a 125-mile diameter crater, known as 'The Bedout High', off the northwest coast of Australia. The second was an asteroid impact of enormous proportions, better known for wiping-out the dinosaurs about sixty-five million years ago. It landed in Chicxulub, an area of the Mexican Yucatan Peninsula; it formed a crater some five hundred miles in diameter, forming what is now the Bay of Mexico. Both not only threw up dust and debris that blocked-out the sunlight for many, many years, but also caused a massive ripple of the earth's crust, triggering intense volcanic activity and the release of poisonous methane gas, in pockets since the Carboniferous Period, which added to the chaos.

The other four events were variously attributed to extensive ice ages, the eruption of huge super-volcanoes, and /or the further release of methane gas, the latter being thought a particular possibility, derived from a study of Siberian geography.

He now spent time studying the next phase of evolution, from Hominids 3.4 million years ago to Homo Sapiens some

30,000 years ago. In thinking about the problem of his presumed date for Adam & Eve, he remembered that when he was looking for the number of years between Adam & Eve and Christ, he had noticed that some of the jobs done by Adam and his offspring were given. So, he returned to the Book of Genesis to see if this would throw any light on his difficulty?

He saw that Adam *'farmed the land'* as did his son Cain, whereas Abel, Adam's second son, *'became a shepherd'*. Looking at his photocopied pages of The Times History of the World, he'd brought from the library, he saw that the very earliest forms of farming only dated from between 7,000 BC and had fairly well evolved by 5,000 BC. This would make it impossible for Adam to be the first of the Hominids, over three million years before. Conversely it would be entirely possible if they were created in 3,926 BC.

Encouraged, he looked further. In the sixth generation after Adam, Jabal was born in 3,304 BC. *'Jabal was the ancestor of those that raise livestock'*. Then, in the next generation came the strongest evidence yet, that his presumption was probably right. Tubal Cain was born in 3,239 BC and the bible read— *'Tubal Cain, who made all kinds of tools out of bronze and iron'*. The first traces of bronze casting in the Near East were dated at around 4,000 BC.

He was now sure that the biblical evidence clearly indicated that his calculated time for Adam & Eve's creation was entirely possible. How on Earth could this be however, when humankind had already been in existence for over three million years?

He had studied evolution, not only to see if it fitted the steps of time, but also in the hope that it would give him a clue to solving the human timing problem as well. It had fitted into the steps of time, but he was no nearer solving the Adam & Eve timing problem. What with this, and the starting date of creation, he was feeling very frustrated.

Chapter Six
Breakthrough

Christopher caught BA 213 for Boston, which left Heathrow at 10.40. He was looking forward to seeing something of America, seeing Thea again, and meeting her father.

The flight dragged a little, he spent his time repeatedly thinking, reading and listening to music, interrupted by lunch and afternoon tea. The film didn't capture his interest either, he could neither settle nor concentrate. By design or coincidence, when he first caught sight of land, which he assumed was Newfoundland, Dvorak's ninth symphony—From the New World, had just started. As he listened, he settled for the first time, heard it afresh, it 'spoke' to him of the America he had not yet seen. It added to his anticipation and was to become a treasured memory of his first visit.

About an hour or so later the engines were throttled back and they began a slow descent. As he began to see built-up areas from a few thousand feet, he noticed the flaps were lowered in stages, with a corresponding rise in power to compensate for the increased drag. He then saw Boston laid out below, when full flap was lowered on final approach to land. There was a screech of rubber as the undercarriage touched the ground—the wheels being jerked up to speed, landing at Boston's Logan Airport at one-thirty local time. He queued at immigration, waited a short while for his suitcase and then met Thea and her father who were waiting. Thea's greeting and embrace were understandably brief and restrained, before introducing him to her father.

They left the airport, driving on the right, like continental Europe. Mr Theurgy explained that after a seven and a half-hour flight and with a five-hour time difference, he would be experiencing jetlag and tiredness from the extended twenty-nine-hour day. Therefore, they'd made no plans for the rest of the day, other than an early evening meal, so he would be free to go to bed when he wished.

When they arrived home in Somerville, Mr Theurgy welcomed him to their home and showed Christopher his room. He unpacked, freshened up and when he went downstairs Thea had made coffee. There was small talk while they drank, Mr Theurgy complimenting him on 'The Three Wise Men' article that Thea had shown him. Then Thea suggested the two of them take a gentle stroll down to the Mystic River to stretch his legs and see a little of Boston. It had been her father's idea really, to give them time to themselves, while he prepared the evening meal.

As they walked, he was taking-in the differences in architectural style, the street signs, and the cars and taxis. She said she'd missed him and how pleased she was that he could come. He explained how the New World Symphony had given him a pleasurable 'insight' into what was to come.

They caught up on what they had been doing. Chris explained his further research at the library, after his return from Brussels and the time spent wrestling with the details. He had finally worked out how to fit it all into the steps of time, but he was unable to progress on the real issue, how to reconcile the time difference between the arrival of humans and the creation of Adam & Eve.

Thea said she had a surprise for him on that score, "but dad made me promise I wouldn't tell you until the three of us are together. He feels he's missed out on our investigation so far and he wants to take part. I do hope you understand?"

"Yes of course, after all, he organised the initial translation, but you've got me intrigued."

"Dad's mad keen to discuss the document and the details of progress so far, you did bring it didn't you?"

"Yes, I'll get it from my case when we get back."

When they got back, Chris got the document and showed it to her father.

"This is real special, I never thought I'd ever see anything quite like this, I suppose you know it's real? I feel very humble to have it in my hands!"

"Yes" said Chris, "I've come to believe so too, it took me a while to reach that conclusion. I shied away from the idea initially saying, 'it can't be for me'? I agree—it makes one feel humble. It's a great challenge."

"It sure does, let's discuss how you're been getting on over our meal; it's ready." Saying that, he brought in the meal.

When they were seated, Mr Theurgy said, "You British are so formal—I'd much prefer it if you'd call me Manny. Yes, Thea is named after me, the female version of course, but here in the States, Manny is quite a popular name." He then said grace. As they ate, Thea dropped her bombshell.

She explained she'd had time on her hands at the flat, before leaving for Boston. She decided to read Genesis yet again, to see if a new light would dawn on the human timing problem? She'd decided to keep what she'd discovered as a surprise until Chris' arrival. She felt she needed the time to think it through before telling either of them.

"I think I've found the answer to the human timing problem."

"You have!" said Chris.

"Well, I think it could go a long way to explaining it." She continued: "Bearing in mind the statement by God *I will make human beings,* I found, when I got to chapter two, verse seven, a marked change, it read, *...he breathed life-giving breath into his nostrils and man began to live.* I registered the word *man* was used in place of human beings, do you see, *man* came after the words, *breathed life-giving breath.* Then later, in chapter five in fact, it became clearer still, quite explicit really, it read, *...He made them like himself. He created them male and female, blessed them, and named them* 'Mankind'.

A real change had occurred that couldn't just be a foible of translation. There is a clear distinction between *human beings* in the earlier text and *man,* then later, *Mankind,* in the later text. Thinking about it afterwards, I concluded that God had fashioned human beings *from the soil* first, and only later, when they were sufficiently developed, did he give them a soul to make them *like himself.*

From what you've explained Chris, I concluded that Mankind was only created when humankind had been made ready for that final step of creation. That is, after the evolutionary development of Hominids, Homo Erectus and Homo Sapiens were completed. Only then did God create Mankind by giving human beings a soul (*life-giving breath*) a spiritual dimension to their being (*like himself*).

"Thea, I think that's fantastic, I think you've found the answer. I see I'll have to start reading the bible a lot more carefully from now on. What do you think Manny?

"She's always been a bright girl Chris, just explain what your problem was Chris?"

As Chris explained to her father, Thea thought about what Chris said he'd been doing during their walk. When Chris had finished, she said:

"When we were out walking Chris, and you were explaining about Adam farming around 5,000 BC or later, and, was it Tubal Cain. Who produced things in bronze which must have been around 4,000 BC or after. I said to myself, it all seems to fit with my discovery."

They continued their conversation; Chris getting to know Manny and vice versa, as he and Thea brought Manny up to date on all they had been able to deduce so far, until Chris retired to bed.

Chris woke quite early next morning, not yet acclimated to the new time; he understood it normally took two to three days. He went quietly downstairs, so as not to disturb them, and noticed a couple of maps on the table. It seemed that Thea and her father had been talking about what they might do.

He picked one up that covered Connecticut, Massachusetts and Rhode Island. He marvelled at the fact that each was divided from the other almost entirely by straight lines and very little by geographical features. When he looked around the Boston area he could see why it was called New England. There were so many recognisable place names—Cambridge of course, Braintree, Weymouth, and Wakefield. Slightly further away, Gloucester, Newbury, Ipswich and still further, Plymouth, Falmouth and many others.

Chris was thinking about Thea's observation of the biblical wording, humankind to mankind, when she came downstairs some while later. They greeted each other warmly then started to get breakfast, she explained that her father would soon be down. Over breakfast they explained to Chris what they had planned for today; soon after breakfast they left.

First down to the harbour to visualise the 'Tea Party' where they also explained there was a backwater of the harbour, and an area of the city, called Chelsea. In addition to the Mystic River, the Charles River also emptied into the harbour. They then headed south to Plymouth to visit the replica Mayflower and then see how the Plymouth Brethren lived when they first landed at the Plymouth plantation.

They carried on south to Falmouth and caught a ferry to Martha's Vineyard, having a late lunch of the biggest pizza Christopher had ever seen. After lunch, they went on a conducted tour of the island, then made their way home, retracing the route back to Somerville.

While Thea and her father busied themselves with getting an evening meal, Chris had a look at an American newspaper for the first time—The Boston Herald. An article caught his eye—a team at the Rowland Institute, here in Cambridge Massachusetts, had succeeded in slowing down light.

There was a report from the American Association for the Advancement of Science. In summary it said—Professor Lene Hau's team had shown that the speed of light could be slowed to a 'crawl'. In the experiment, they had reduced the temperature of sodium atoms, chilled them down to one-millionth of a degree above absolute zero. At this point the atoms merge to form, what is called, a 'Bose-Einstein' condensate. Once the condensate is created, a 'coupling' laser, tuned to resonate with the trapped mass of atoms is beamed into the trap-chamber so that the atoms and photons of light become 'entangled'. A pulsed laser probe was then shot into the 'laser-dressed' condensate from a different laser—it was the latter light that was slowed to a "crawl" from its normal 186,000 miles per second.

Christopher's excitement rose as he read the article, recalling his thinking on the way back from Brussels. Here, for the first time, was an experiment that proved that the speed of light was not necessarily a constant, as had been stated by Einstein—it could change, or be made to change! The germ of an idea, possibly the solution to the sixteen billion-year question, beckoned him.

Over dinner he did his best to explain the importance of this finding. He went on to say that from Einstein's theory of relativity, and the many experiments that had confirmed it, the speed of light was a constant datum in the universe. This new experiment could have many implications for physics, astronomy, and many other aspects of science.

He told them about the 'Universe' TV programme he had seen, in it, an American with a name that sounded like Macuizo or Macuso, had suggested that the speed of light had possibly slowed over aeons of time. His reasoning, Christopher recalled, was that an equation, or equations, covering the 'Big Bang' theory of creation had some glitches, as he called them. If one assumed that the speed of all radiation, initially travelled significantly faster than its present speed, then the glitches would disappear. This idea has not been given much credence, as all modern scientists had been raised on the fact that Einstein's theory of relativity said the speed of light was an absolute and invariable constant. Many subsequent experiments had confirmed this aspect of the theory.

But now, for the first time, here was an experiment, which showed that the speed of light could in fact change. If his germ of an idea was right, this new research could solve the date of creation problem. Chris felt he needed to understand Macuso's position as a starting point, was there any chance he could meet up with him while he was here?

After some debate it was agreed that Manny would take Chris to the museum and other places of interest in Boston tomorrow. Thea would stay home and work the phone to try and locate this Macuso character. If she did, she would see if a meeting were possible.

Manny and Chris had a good day out and got to know each other much better. Over lunch they talked about the work of the Peabody Museum, compared rugby with American football, and Manny tried to explain baseball. After lunch, they visited the Rowland Institute and Manny showed Chris the Radcliffe College where Thea studied, on the way home in mid-afternoon.

When they got in Thea was excited by her success. She had traced Macuzio to California; he was coming to Washington on Sunday for a convention next week. With the time difference, he would be late arriving, but if Chris could meet him in the hotel, say 10:00 Monday morning, he would be happy to spend an hour or two, as delegate registration was 12:00 to 13:00 to allow for 'local' arrivals.

"How did you manage all that?" Chris asked.

"I'll have you know I'm not just a pretty face. No, really, it's an unusual name and AT&T was most helpful. I ended up only making eleven calls before I found the right one."

"How on Earth did you get him to see me?"

"Well, from what you'd told me, my impression was that nobody's pursuing his ideas. He's a bit frozen out in the astronomical world, maybe, for questioning Einstein's theory, even if it is only in part, but I'm guessing. I flattered him a little, then said we had a young Englishman of twenty-two staying with us, who remembered seeing him on a BBC science programme. He's studying at Cambridge, doing math and physics under Stephen Hawking, aiming to get a double first and become an astrophysicist. He has an open mind and would like to clearly understand his ideas about the speed of light."

"Sounds like you laid it on a bit, I hope I can live up to the billing and follow what he says when I get there."

"Why don't you and Thea go and do some sightseeing while you're there?" Manny said. "Fly down to Washington National and take a look at the White House and some of the Smithsonian as well."

"I know," said Thea. "We'll go to mass Saturday evening and fly down to Baltimore Washington International Airport Sunday morning. I can take Chris to Towson and show him a bit of Baltimore—Harbour Place in particular and then we can drive down to Washington Sunday evening. After your meeting on Monday we can do what dad suggests and fly back from Washington National."

This was agreed, so Thea went ahead with the flight and hotel bookings, Chris insisting that she use his credit card.

They had a quiet morning on Saturday. Manny said he would find out the times of the Episcopalian services, explaining that's what the Anglicans call themselves here, but Chris said not to bother, he would like to come to mass with them.

Chris took them out to lunch at one of their favourite restaurants, and they walked it off in Hammond Pond Park.

When they were home, after mass, Manny raised the question of Chris's reaction to female priests and the problem of homosexuality that was splitting the Anglican community. Chris said that he and his sister had discussed this on a number of occasions, and with their parents. They were upset over the question of female vicars, but all four of them were very sickened by the homosexual question. As yet no one had suggested they consider making a change, although he was sure it was in the back of all their minds. "To be honest, I've been so busy at Cambridge, I hadn't thought about it again until quite recently, until the events at Stonehenge in fact."

They were up early on Sunday morning and Manny took them to Logan Airport. After he and Thea landed at Baltimore/Washington International, they drove as planned. Chris was impressed with Harbour Place, where they had lunch. Then they drove out to Towson; Chris was fascinated to see how the town was spread out compared to England, there seemed to be so much space. They had a look at the Theurgy's previous single-storey house in Pott Spring Road, and finally took the I-95 to Washington.

They had a quiet meal in the hotel, talking of Towson, Baltimore, his impressions of America so far, and a little of what tomorrow's meeting might bring. They had brought a map and went to Chris's room to plan the route to Macuzio's hotel, their sightseeing in the afternoon and the route out to Washington National Airport, at the side of the Potomac River.

They both realised that they got on extremely well together and were happy in each other's company. Their relationship had grown close in the few weeks since they'd met. This expressed itself when Thea got up to go to her room, saying good night. They found themselves in a tight embrace, kissing passionately. They mutually broke away; each shocked by the moment, each conscious of their earlier resolve. Thea left, subdued, not saying another word.

They were still subdued in the restaurant at breakfast the following morning. Each having had difficulty getting to sleep and having spent a restless night thinking of how they felt about each other. With the imminent Macuzio meeting, they recognised that now was not the time, nor was it the place, to discuss their feelings.

They drove to Macuzio's hotel and parked. They had agreed she would wait in the lobby, maybe have a coffee and begin a book she'd bought at the airport the previous day. Chris went to reception and asked for Mr Macuzio's room, saying he was expected.

Chris went up to room 809, after reception had phoned through to announce his arrival. As he approached the room, he saw that Mr Macuzio had already opened his door and was waiting at the entrance to greet him.

While Mr Macuzio phoned room service for coffee, Chris explained that ever since the BBC programme he was intrigued with Macuzio's idea. Now he was at Cambridge, with two years to go he wished to explore the possibility of expanding on Macuzio's idea for his doctoral thesis, if he had no objection.

Mr Macuzio said he was quite keen for a new, vigorous young mind to address the question. His thinking had not been pursued; his peers felt the idea too radical. They believed Einstein's Relativity—the speed of light was a proven universal datum, Macuzio's thinking must be wrong. He was not sure they were right, so then went on to start to explain how he had reached his doubts.

They sat alongside each other at the desk in the bedroom, as Macuzio took him through his thinking. Chris was just able to stay with the concepts to which he was being exposed. Equations filled sheet after sheet and Chris began to see how and why Macuzio had come to question one aspect of Einstein's assertion. Chris had some difficulties, at his elevated level of maths, but Macuzio became like a teacher, expanding Chris's mind to new insights of cosmology.

They worked at it for almost two hours before the questions dried up, coming to a natural close. Chris expressed his heartfelt gratitude, asked if he might keep all the working papers to study. He came down to the lobby where Chris promised he would keep in touch regarding his progress, if any. Macuzio then left them to join his fellow delegates to register and go in for lunch. He was silently impressed with the intelligence of Chris's questions and his quick grasp of new concepts, in a young man of twenty-two. He felt the problem was in capable hands, particularly as his formal education still had some way to go.

As the delegates were filling the restaurant, Chris and Thea decided to go back to their hotel for lunch. Chris was understandably preoccupied, mulling over Macuzio's ideas, but he made an effort for Thea's sake. There was a tacit understanding that last evening's event should be left for now while they enjoyed an afternoon of sightseeing.

They had a look at the White House and Capitol Building, but ended up spending most time in the aerospace museum of the Smithsonian before they made their way to the airport for their return flight. Manny was there to meet them and by the time they a got home it was quite late.

Manny asked how Chris's meeting had gone, so he repeated what he'd told Thea on the plane. He was quietly confident that his discussion had opened the door to his eight billion number being the start of the universe. It would take a great deal of effort to prove it in the face of the entrenched position of the establishment. In fact, he considered it could take him all of his remaining two years, he would have to be absolutely sure he was right. If he convinced himself, he envisaged presenting it as his doctoral thesis.

The following morning at breakfast, Manny told them he had booked a summer concert at the Boston Symphony Hall for all of them that evening, as Chris was due to leave the following evening. Chris said he would like to catch up a bit on his notes about Adam & Eve, but more particularly his meeting with Macuzio. He suggested to Thea it might be nice to see a bit more of Boston maybe stroll along by the Charles River in the afternoon.

Over lunch, which Thea had prepared, Chris referred to his note making, by saying: "Until I started making notes, I hadn't realised the implications of Adam & Eve being created as late as 3926 BC before. Humankind had already spread a long way across the Earth by that date. Therefore Adam & Eve could only have been the first of Mankind as far as the

Jewish race are concerned—the first of their ancestors, as told in the bible. What I'm saying is, that Adam & Eve happen to be the only people on record, who represent the step-change that took place, from Homo Sapiens to Mankind. Lost documents, if any, in other parts of the world, might equally have recorded the creation of Mankind in other countries, races, or religions." I concluded that the creation of Mankind by God must have been a global act.

"That's a good point" said Manny. "I wanted to tell you, over breakfast, what I'd been up to while you two were away, but you both seemed a bit quiet and it is a bit heavy for first thing."

"That's thoughtful of you dad, it sounds a bit ominous."

"No, not at all, it's just a bit complex. Our reasoning about humankind, mankind and Adam and Eve might be satisfactory for us, but people at large think of them as the very first people. They have probably never considered a distinction between humankind and mankind; they're all the same to them—just people. I don't think we can prove what we are saying, but I felt we must do the next best thing, show that it's more than likely.

"So far, we've only found two pointers indicating what happened, but neither is what one might call positive proof. To find— *'will make human beings'* is interesting. The second pointer— *'human beings,* later changing to *man',* then on to *'mankind',* makes it much more probable. But I felt we needed a third; we could then hypothesise with significantly more confidence if we had three distinct references, it would make the case more convincing."

Chris and Thea looked at each other, then said, almost the same thing: "I can see what you mean."

"To cut a long story short. On Sunday, after you'd left, I eventually found another reference in the letter to the Hebrews, chapter two, verse six. It relies on one's interpretation of the meaning. It says... *As it is said somewhere in the Scriptures: 'You made him for a little while lower than the angels; you crowned him with glory and honour.'*

"I felt that it indicated there were two phases of creation, *You made him **for a little while** lower than the angels* (Hominids, Homo Erectus and Homo Sapiens) and then, *you crowned him with glory and honour.* Here was another distinction between humankind and mankind?"

"It would seem so," said Chris.

I thought I should find the other element to which it refers *somewhere in the Scriptures.* After much searching, I finally found it in psalm eight, verse five. *Yet you made him inferior only to yourself; you crowned him with glory and honour.* My hopes of further clarification were dashed, the crucial phrase, *for a little while,* or something similar, is missing is I needed help.

Our Mary Nodar, the woman who translated your document, is visiting the National Library in London at the moment. I felt she would know, or could probably find out, whom to contact, to see if this anomaly between the two verses could be resolved.

I emailed her Sunday evening and her reply was on the computer this morning, so I'm glad I didn't talk about it at breakfast. I printed off two copies, here they are.

I got a lucky break, your query, particularly the apparent omission, sure stirred a few minds. One of the library's prize possessions is a copy of *Codex Sinaiticus,* a 4th-century biblical manuscript. I was able to refer to it with one of their professors here; he was very intrigued by your question.

We looked carefully at the *Codex* text of the eighth psalm and found we were in something of a dilemma. Our interpretation did not wholly agree with current translations. We discussed the nuances at length, as a result we agreed that the translation should read something like, *Yet, you made him without a spirit, then you crowned him with glory, etc.*

We felt it was too important to rely on ourselves alone, so we consulted with two eminent colleagues. We phoned them—one in Jerusalem, the other in Baghdad, would you believe?

They agreed that *without a spirit* or *without spirit* was valid. We are all familiar with how it could have been translated as either *inferior only to yourself* or *less than the angels.* It's one of the common problems that arise from ancient texts. In some cases they have been translated from translations of the original text, as they spread from culture to culture and language to language. Additionally, the person doing the translation can inadvertently introduce a nuance, conditioned as they are by their own local language and culture.

Perhaps more importantly from your point of view, they found your interpretation of the text, i.e. the evolution to humankind, later transformed into 'Mankind', very interesting. Quite a revolutionary idea really, but they felt it was not inconsistent with the original psalm or the letter to the Hebrews.

After Thea read it, she thanked her father in a roundabout way, saying, "You must have spent a lot of time finding them, and thinking about it dad. But the endorsement of recognised authorities on the subject is invaluable, it sure adds credence to the idea, don't you think so Chris?"

"Yes, I like it. The bible has finesse in making its point.

"So," Manny said, "like the other two pointers, it's not entirely clear-cut, but it's enough of an endorsement for me, I'm satisfied we can argue our case with a high level of assurance."

As they strolled alongside the Charles River bank, Christopher raised the subject that had been in the back of their minds for almost two days. "I was shocked with the unexpected suddenness and intensity of our embrace the evening before last. It seemed to come from nowhere, and I understood why you left. I spent ages calming down and trying to get to sleep. I kept turning it over in my mind; it ended up as a very restless night."

"Me too Chris—my desire was suddenly so intense I could hardly bear it, I've never felt like that before. I've thought about little else since, I tossed and turned all night as well. To me it seemed like a test, could I control my emotions? You have at least another two years to do at university. I would hate to upset your studies, I want you to achieve a double first and obtaining a doctorate is the most important thing you can do. I know in my bones you are capable of going a long way, I want to help, not hinder you."

"I'm glad you feel like that" Chris relied, "I promised myself, and my parents that my studies would come first. I want to have built a solid foundation to my life before I marry. I'd no idea that our friendship would blossom this far in so few weeks. Perhaps it's as you say, it was some kind of test, our rapport over the document has a lot to answer for."

"Chris, it may sound old fashioned, but I promised myself I would be a virgin for my husband on my wedding night. I almost gave in to my feelings for you the other night, it shook me, that's why I walked out without a word, I couldn't explain. No offence, but I want to keep my resolve. I like you a great deal Chris, but let's concentrate on the document as friends, not lovers?"

"Thea, you came into my life, almost unbidden as it were. I've come to value your friendship very highly indeed. I too made a resolution when we were in Brussels; I wanted you even then. I have a great deal of respect for you, you're beautiful, but I don't want to debase how I feel about you. I want to be sensible, I'd like to remain close friends if it's possible, but I must be single-minded about my studies. If our friendship lasts, and I think it will, let's see how we feel when I've finished my studies."

"I'm so glad you feel the same way Chris, I think we should guard against getting ourselves into that kind of situation again, don't you?"

"Yes, I'm pleased we've cleared up how we feel it's nice to know we are of similar minds. The tension between us has gone; I feel our mutual understanding has strengthened our friendship."

They enjoyed the concert and Manny noticed, during the evening, how much more relaxed was their relationship, it seemed to have matured during the week. He liked Chris a great deal; from their discussions surrounding the document, he guessed his IQ bordered on genius. Combined with his friendly personality he foresaw Chris going far. If Thea had the patience and gave the friendship time to evolve, he would make a fine husband one day.

Christopher took them both out to lunch the following day, to thank them for their hospitality. He was flying back overnight on BA212, leaving at 6:05 pm. They talked about his meeting with Macuzio and their own discoveries that had advanced their understanding of the document.

Chris said he would probably spend the rest of the holiday incorporating these ideas into a summary document. No doubt Thea would keep her father advised of progress, but Chris also promised to stay in touch.

He had enjoyed what he had seen of America, but didn't know if or when he might see Manny again. He was quite happy to be leaving, wanting to make progress on the document. Also knowing that Thea would be following him the coming weekend. He told them of Helen's imminent departure for Thailand and passed on his mother's invitation for Thea to come for the weekend after her return.

Chapter Seven
Insight

Helen had agreed to meet Christopher on his return from Boston at the unearthly hour of 5:30 am. Mum and dad were committed to their respective schools to begin preparations for the new term. Helen was prepared to do this in case the flight was delayed, and because they had not seen a great deal of each other this holiday. She was due to leave on Saturday for her extended visit to Thailand.

They gave each other a good hug when he emerged from the customs hall. As they walked to the car park, he said he'd had a good holiday, but was pleased to be home. As she drove out of Heathrow onto the M4, Helen explained she would drop him off at home, then do some 'final' visiting while he caught up on his sleep. She'd be back mid-afternoon, as she'd agreed to cook the evening meal for them all.

Christopher was up when Helen returned, in fact he was in the middle of making some tea, American coffee was fine, but tea was something he'd really missed. As they sat enjoying their tea, Helen asked Chris about Thea. She was slightly intrigued; none of the family had met her, yet he'd spent time with her in Brussels and now Boston.

Chris explained it was Thea's involvement in the document that had brought them together, but the relationship had deepened. "Don't take this the wrong way, but these last few weeks we have become really good friends. I wouldn't find it difficult to fall in love with her, she's lovely, but I'm conscious that I've got two more years at Cambridge and she clearly understands this is my priority."

"Mum told me she's asked you to invite her, I understand she's coming for the weekend after this. I'm sorry I'll miss her, but no doubt mum will write and tell me all about her."

Over dinner that evening Chris told them about his holiday. His impression of Boston, his trip to the 'Mayflower', Falmouth and Martha's Vineyard. He talked of his discussions with Mr Theurgy about the document. Thea's contribution to the human timing problem by making a clear distinction between humankind and Mankind in Genesis, his mother was most impressed. He also explained Manny's additional contribution from the letter to the Hebrews and the eighth psalm.

He talked about how excited he was with the speed of light experiment and being able to meet up with Mr Macuzio in Washington. How this presented a great challenge for him to clearly understand on his return to Cambridge. He also mentioned the opportunity this gave for sightseeing in Baltimore and Washington—Harbour Place, the White House, the Capitol, the Lincoln Memorial and the Smithsonian.

He wasn't tired when they all went to bed, so he got out the human timing notes he'd made in the States and the photocopies of the charts from 'The Living Planet' as well as those from the two books on human evolution.

Christopher thought how best to tackle the revisions he needed to make now that the human/mankind timing problem was resolved. He decided to address it in reverse, so to speak. He would assume that 'Day Six' lasted until Adam & Eve were created in 3926 BC, almost six thousand years ago.

Turning to his 'steps of time chart' and ignoring the sixteen billion-year number, day six would have started in step six of time. Counting up the number of steps to the year 3926 BC came to a further fifteen. Suddenly he saw it—why hadn't he seen it before? In the planet reference, this was days one to six of creation, with day six having fifteen steps. Mankind was then created and Christ was born at the end of step twenty-one! He dropped off to sleep, happy in the knowledge that it all made sense.

Mum had taken the day off to help Helen pack and get ready for her journey; Chris retired to the study. In laying out the timing, he started from where he'd left it, prior to going to America at the end of day five. He realised he could now use the additional datum point, the historically established date for the emergence of Hominids—circa 3.4 million years ago.

He established that day six started with the Triassic Period at the beginning of the Mesozoic Era and ran right through to the Holocene Epoch in the Quaternary Period of the Cenozoic Era. It took him some considerable time to sort it all out until finally he was pleasantly surprised at how well it all came together.

It took the first six steps of time in day six to complete the geography and climate of the world. The same six steps to complete the flora, and fauna of the world, the latter being 'Chad Toumai'- the immediate forebear of the Hominids. It then took the remaining nine steps of time to steer the evolutionary path, from 'Chad Toumai' into the three phases of human development, Hominids, Homo Erectus and Homo Sapiens. Homo Sapiens finally reaching the pinnacle of development, the point where God chose to create Mankind!

When he reviewed what he had done he thought, what else in addition could the scribe of Genesis have said about those first six steps of day six that he did not say? It was simply the continued evolution of flora and fauna, to bring God's earlier commands to fruition. Similarly, what could usefully have been added to Genesis regarding the evolution of humankind over the ensuing nine steps? There was no reason to doubt, as a result of mankind's research, that these events occurred. He also reflected on the fact that Thea's interpretive insight of the bible's content enabled it, and Darwin's theory of evolution, to be reconciled. The document's provenance was complete, subject to the speed of light.

Christopher had a light lunch with Helen and his mother; they would have a family farewell dinner for Helen this evening, when Eugene was home. After lunch, he returned to the study to make notes of his thoughts about the speed of light.

He knew for the first time, from the report on the speed of light experiment that the speed of light could alter. He'd suspected this might be possible when he thought about Macuzio's original claim in the TV programme, his discussions had added to this belief. Macuzio, and the experiment, gave him the leeway and motivation he needed to further develop the idea he'd had on the train from Brussels.

The way the document finally came together illustrated that his idea, about the change in the speed of light, must be so. It was no proof positive that he could lay in front of his peers, they wanted scientific argument and proof, nothing less. He would start his endeavours by listing his reasons as the starting point for his endeavours.

Professor Hawking had pulled together many ideas, from among his peers, when he hit upon the concept that the universe started from a singularity. He reversed the process through which we now believed a Black Hole is created. He ended up with the 'Big Bang' theory.

The original singularity must have had a density beyond imagining; it contained everything that is in the universe. The Black Holes that have been identified in the current universe are so dense that even the speed of light is below their escape velocity. This illustrates that even light has a mass, albeit minute. This conclusion is confirmed by the fact that light is bent by extremes of gravity, the apparent shift of stars by microlensing through space. The escape velocity of the energy released by the explosion of the original, massive singularity, must therefore have been a number of times faster than the current speed of light, otherwise it would have collapsed back in upon itself.

The enormous gravitational pull however, slowed this energy down over time, the process by which it was transformed into hydrogen—the fundamental building block of the universe. Once the production of hydrogen was complete, all residual radiation stabilised at the present speed of light.

His next point arose from the famous American astronomer Edwin Hubble. Hubble had developed the theory of the expanding universe from observing the red shift in light from ever more distant galaxies—the Doppler effect. This led to what became known as the Hubble Constant, or Hubble's

Law. That is, the velocity of a galaxy is proportional to its distance in the expanding universe.

Christopher's contention was bold. Like many 'intuitive' steps, it was driven by the document, born out of a young uncluttered mind and derived from a simple overview. He was not yet sufficiently schooled, or immersed in scientific detail, to pre-condition his thinking. He simply saw the Hubble Constant from a different perspective, in a completely different light, so to speak.

His logic was this. If the speed of the energy released in the Big Bang was significantly faster initially, but then slowed over time, Hubble's observations would be exactly the same. The observable 'horizon' of the universe is currently about fourteen to fifteen billion light years away. The light now reaching a telescope from there, is therefore fourteen to fifteen billion years old.

Objects on the horizon were generated at a time when the universe was expanding much faster than it is now, perhaps much, much faster. So the nearer the galaxy, the younger the age of the light reaching the observer the slower the speed of expansion had become. When one gets to the 'local group' as the nearest galaxies are called, there is no observable red shift.

Light is yet another form of radiation, that subsequently evolved, and its speed, as Einstein rightly predicted, has become a fixed datum. We now know that it can be changed, therefore had light existed in the spectrum of radiation at the time of the Big Bang its speed would have been the same as every other form of radiant energy. This being the case, then the universe could easily be quite a lot younger than previously thought.

The key is, that using the speed of light as the yardstick; the universe is thought to be about 16 billion years old. If, as Macuizo hypothesised, the speed of all radiant energy was much faster originally, then the size of the universe could be quite different, even larger than currently thought, yet its age could be 8.2 billion years. This would account for the unexpected fact that complete galaxies have been photographed on the 'horizon', near what observers had believed, was close to the beginning of the universe.

Hubble's red shift accounts for a speed of expansion that is only a fraction of the speed of light. Therefore, the universe might conceivably have ceased to expand, be in a steady state, or perhaps have even begun to contract. The light we are seeing is so old; we cannot know the current status of the universe. The possibility of contraction, back into a Black Hole, seems to be favoured as an ever-repeating cyclical event over many aeons of time, by Professor Hawking.

This all seemed logical to Christopher, although it undoubtedly flew in the face of all current cosmological thinking. He rationalised his idea, without any sense of ego, by thinking that once upon a time, the universe was said to revolve around the Earth, but later mankind discovered, it didn't. He also recalled that Lord Kelvin had deduced the age of the Earth to be about 20 million years, based on heat loss. Once the heat generated by radioactive decay entered the equation, the lifespan calculation changed dramatically. There were, no doubt, many other examples.

His belief in the authenticity of the document satisfied him that his conjecture might be somewhere near the truth. While it would be a hard task, he was determined to see if he could prove it to be the case. The subsequent minute scrutiny of his peers was also a daunting prospect. He had said, on the spur of the moment in America, that it might take him two years. His meeting with Macuzio showed him that he had a long way to go, it could well take him that, or more.

On checking his emails, there was one from Thea. She told him she was coming back to England, arriving Sunday morning, on the same flight he'd taken the previous Wednesday. She'd go direct to Hammersmith and spend the week catching up with things at the flat and doing some work in London.

She would ring him when she was back and was looking forward to seeing him and meeting his parents on Friday. She was sorry to miss Helen, but asked him to pass on her best wishes for her holiday and hoped she would enjoy her work in Thailand.

All three went to Heathrow with Helen on Saturday, there were some tears, but they all promised to stay in touch by email, letter and phone. They wished her a good holiday and hoped the work in the Pattaya orphanage would feel rewarding and be enjoyable.

Having made the notes of his conjecture about the formation of the universe, he now reviewed the pages of Macuzio's illustrative workings in Washington. He had no option but to leave the topic for the time being, he could go no further at the moment, but was armed with an additional purpose when returning to his studies at Cambridge.

Putting that aside, the end of his holiday was fast approaching, just two weeks left. He felt it would be right to consolidate his understanding of the document's provenance by writing a complete summary of what he now understood. This would not only be for his file, but he would give it to all who had helped his understanding. His mother had clarified the 'Current Status' with her biblical quotes, he would do likewise with the 'Location' and timing.

He would do it this coming week, make it a small present to the family and Thea next weekend; a thank-you gesture for their help and support

His filed copy would aid his memory and set the backdrop to the 'Remedial Action Decrees' of the twenty-third step of time, which he would have to come back to at a later date.

Chapter Eight
The First Twenty-One Steps of Time

This Document is to thank you all for your invaluable contributions to solving the mystery of "The Document."

It is not a story to read, but more a reference document incorporating all we have learnt from solving the first half of "The Document". It incorporates all that we have learnt as an abridged "Book of Genesis", with one additional assumption on my part.

I have assumed I will be able to prove to my peers that the speed of light has changed—creation therefore started with the "Big Bang" some eight billion years ago, instead of some 16 billion.

My love and thanks
Chris

"CREATION"
See Appendix Three

Chapter Nine
Headway

Christopher and Thea had spoken on the phone, since her return from Boston. So they met at Boulter's Lock car park on Friday afternoon, where she left her car. Christopher was once again taken by surprise at her beauty and complimented her on how beautiful she looked. From there they went to the Blue River Cafe, overlooking the river, for afternoon tea. As they watched the heavier summertime river traffic plying the Thames, they reminisced about their time in America and caught up on each other's recent activities.

He then took her to Cookham to see the paintings in the Spencer gallery. He left her for a short time to pop across the road to the Bel & Dragon, to book a Saturday evening table for four. When they had finished enjoying Spencer's work, they walked along the riverbank, leaving his car in the moor car park. A little tired, but very happy in each other's company, they finally collected Thea's car and she followed him to his home.

Christopher proudly introduced Thea to his parents; it was pleasing to each of them, as they noticed Eugene and Pat's favourable reaction to Thea. Christopher had brought in her overnight case from her car and his mother showed her up to her room and left her to unpack and freshen up for dinner. While the two ladies were upstairs Eugene commented, "I can certainly see why you wanted to get to know her Chris, she's quite lovely isn't she?"

Over dinner Thea was surprisingly relaxed and confident as the conversation flowed, while they got to know each other. She talked of her childhood in Towson, her time at university, her mother and father and her current one-off assignment doing research across Europe. Eugene and Pat told stories of Christopher's upbringing and their hopes and aspirations for both he and his sister Helen. They talked of the document and her father's keen interest in the progress Christopher had made. Over coffee he handed each of them a nicely prepared presentation folder, saying, "It's a slightly revised and extended version of Creation, based on the early part of Genesis. I posted one each to Manny and Helen this morning. I've booked to take you to dinner tomorrow as a thank you for all your help."

As each of them opened the presentation folders, there was a hand written note at the front, addressed to each, saying, "Thanks (Thea, Mum, Dad) for contributing to the solutions that determined the provenance of the document, I hope you enjoy reading it."

As a foursome they went to Windsor on Saturday to see the changing of the guard and to show Thea round Windsor Castle. They hadn't been for quite a while themselves and were pleasantly surprised at the improvements. Thea was impressed with the number and array of nationalities of the tourists, some, by their accents, very obviously from the USA. She marvelled at what she saw, particularly the age of some things, as she learnt a little of English history, there was just nothing to compare in the States.

They all enjoyed a beautiful meal together at the Bel & Dragon that evening, with some good wine, and returned home quite late and quite mellow. It was pleasing to Chris that his parents did not just accept Thea as his girlfriend, but that they seemed to genuinely like her, like her quite a lot.

Sunday morning Chris accompanied Thea to mass at St Josephs, a Victorian built church of 1884, while his parents went to the Anglican service at St Luke's. After mass he and Thea went for a walk in Maidenhead Thicket while his parents returned home to prepare for lunch.

When they returned home, they discovered that Pat had decided on a typically English lunch of roast beef, baked potatoes and Yorkshire pudding. The sweet course was a surprise however; a peach and Champagne Russie.

Thea was reluctant to leave after they'd spent time chatting over coffee, but she had to prepare for going to Zurich, for at least a week, early the following morning. As she was leaving Pat said she must try to come again, they'd love to have her when Chris was home for the Christmas break and before she went back to the USA, if possible.

On Monday, mum and dad were now full time at their respective schools. They were preparing for the new intake of students when the new academic year started on Thursday. Christopher's New Year started the following week.

He started to review all his working papers relating to the document. He spent considerable time refreshing his mind with Macuzio's working papers once again, ensuring he clearly understood as much as possible. He placed them in a folder to take to Cambridge at the coming weekend. He also made a photocopy of The Document, which he placed, at the front of the same folder, for reference purposes.

On Tuesday he finished reviewing and filing the rest of the papers and casually turned his mind back to the document. The second half of the document listed ten Remedial Actions, Decreed for the Twenty-Third Phase of time. The 1960-start date was one of the two data he'd used to calculate the steps of time; it actually referred to 1954 on the Earth's calendar. He noted that the first of the actions decreed was to 'Increase agricultural output to ten billion level'.

He decided, knowing next to nothing about agriculture, that he would visit his grandparents at their Oxfordshire farm and discuss the topic. He knew they'd be pleased to see him, as he hadn't seen them this holiday. Doing this would give him a start, and perhaps some encouragement, for when he got round to thinking about the implications of the decrees that were to come.

The Wednesday visit went well. His grandparents were now retired, but still lived in the farmhouse, employing a manager to run the farm. They were aware of the document from previous visits by his parents and were happy to help him. His grandfather said he would be pleased to make some notes for Christopher over the next month or so and send them to him.

Christopher returned to university, determined to pursue his outline idea about the initial phase of creation. He was convinced of the fact that the initial speed had to be way in excess of the speed of light. It was conceivable that light itself was also much faster initially. It was a debatable point in his mind whether, by the time light was created, the production of hydrogen in the universe had, or had not ceased.

Armed with the knowledge from the Macuzio discussion, which in some ways were beyond his current years or learning, he took every opportunity to ask his maths or physics lecturers searching questions. Whenever he felt they touched on a point that he thought could impact on this fundamental question, he would ask for further clarification. On occasions wanting to know what it was that supported the point they were making. On a few occasions, where he thought they might have waffled a bit, or he still did not clearly understand their answer, he made a point of going to see them in their rooms.

He made notes as he went, gaining an insight by small degrees, towards his long-term goal. By the end of the first term his tutors wondered what had got into him. They had discussed Christopher's new found intensity, his absolute need for exactness and his fresh desire to learn, sometimes even the smallest detail. Since he had returned from the summer recess it was as if he had an insight beyond his years, an obsession. If he went on like this there was no doubt he was destined to go a long way.

It was not all-intense learning to the exclusion of all else. On the occasional weekend, particularly if he'd seen an item in the paper that caught his attention, he would go to the library, do a bit of research and make some notes. He spoke to his mother and father, as well as Thea most weekends and during the term he exchanged emails with Helen on a few occasions. Thea came up to Cambridge one weekend in November, around midterm, staying in a local hotel on the Saturday night. But there was no doubt, his mind was focused on learning and moving towards a solution to the fundamental question, how to prove the existence of a speed beyond that of light.

Thea had originally rented the flat in Hammersmith to the end of December, not quite knowing when she would finish her assignment. Christopher came home for the Christmas break on Friday. On Monday he went to Thea's flat to help her with the final bit of packing and loaded it into his car, she had, by then, sold hers. They handed-back the keys to the estate agent and came down to Maidenhead for her to stay for a few days before leaving for Boston on the 21st.

She had expanded on the fact that after Zurich she had worked in Paris and Lisbon. She went back to Boston for the long Thanksgiving weekend, so her father wouldn't have to spend it alone. Then ended her assignment with a visit to Madrid and a few more days in Brussels. She was finally going back to Boston for Christmas and to then find a new job.

During her stay Chris showed her a letter the family had received from Helen, knowing, as a Catholic, she'd be interested to read it.

As you know I am very happy working here, it feels very rewarding and the children are wonderful, I'd just love to bring one home with me if that were possible. I've learnt quite a lot about Thailand and the orphanage in the last three months, I thought you might like to hear about it.

As you're aware Thailand is a Buddhist Kingdom, in fact about 95% Buddhist. Buddhism was founded on human thinking, by Siddhartha Gautama, a dissatisfied Hindu, as long ago as the 6th century BC. Buddha means "the Enlightened One", some might argue it's an idolatrous religion.

Talking as a Christian one can quote the first letter of St Paul to the Thessalonians, in which he wrote, *"When we brought you God's message, you accepted it for what it really is, God's message and not some human thinking."* So, from a Christian standpoint, there are two problems here, one spiritual, and the other temporal. Taking the spiritual first.

Christianity, and Catholicism in particular, was seen as an alien fifth column, a Western Institution challenging Thailand's Buddhist culture. A Catholic nun, Sister Agnes Phila was the last Christian martyr, at 31; she was shot not so long ago, on the 26th December 1940. Things have slowly eased in the 61 years since then, but even now Christians are restricted in their activities.

The Thai Religious Affairs Department introduced a quota system in 1982 for missionaries. Just 400 Catholic and 623 Protestant (all other religious denominations) are allowed in a land of 56 million people. You can easily understand there is still a very long way to go.

The temporal problem is quite shocking. Due to the poor standard of living, particularly in the countryside, many families struggle to raise children. Some run away to the cities, thinking they will get rich, or because of abuse. Some are abandoned; disabled children in particular can make the poverty burden unbearable, one sees beggars in all the towns and cities. The burden is heavy on families because the Thai government is rather slow in its ability to introduce social welfare programmes, particularly for the disabled.

The Pattaya Orphanage Trust, which you support, is actually the main source of funds for not one, but five establishments owned and run by the Redemptorists and the Catholic diocese of Chanthaburi. The church sees this work as an additional means of spreading the faith, by recognition of what it does in the community.

The five establishments currently house some 600 children and young adults. There's the orphanage of course, founded in 1972 when a child was left on Fr. Brennan's doorstep. A school for the blind, a school for the deaf, a vocational school for the disabled, and a street children's centre. The first three are primarily local, but the vocational school for the disabled covers the nation.

The 200 young adults in the latter are being taught a trade, either electronic repairs or computer science. They are from 60 of the 78 provinces across Thailand. Once they qualify, they become wage earners, no longer dependent on others. They are proud to say they were taught at the Redemptorist Vocational School in Pattaya, because the United Nations now uses it as the model for such schools across Southeast Asia. But it is the last of the five establishments, the Street Children's Centre, where the temporal problem is at its worst and the need greatest.

Pattaya expanded from a small fishing village in an unsavoury way, to cater for the American forces during the Vietnamese war. A UNICEF report from last year states that a staggering 200,000 to 400,000 children are employed in Thailand's bars, clubs and brothels, and Pattaya, as a main tourist resort, has more than its share.

It was very difficult in the 90's, when the founder, Fr. Brennan, tried to persuade such children that he was offering them free board, lodging and an education, with no strings attached. You can imagine the ridicule he bore, from the children, their minders and their pimps, but he persevered! The message finally got across; the offer was and is genuine.

There is an ever-present need to save these young children from paedophiles, to take them off the streets before they are mentally scarred for life or end up in an early grave from disease.

In 1997 there were just eight of these children in a house, on loan from a local Catholic of German origin. They then built a home for 150 such children, thinking this to be an optimistic number. They then employed two outreach workers doing the work started by Fr. Brennan. At the year's end, it's pleasing to see that the number has risen from 76 to 81 of these children in residence during the time I've been here.

Your sponsorship of a child, along with the many hundreds of others, is priceless. To quote from the nineteenth psalm, these five forms of charitable work mean, *"No speech, no word, no voice is heard; yet their message goes out to all the world."*

Is this non-verbal message getting across? Well, St Niklaus' church in Pattaya seats 200, it now has seven masses on a Sunday for a regular congregation of just over a thousand. Thai attitudes are slowly changing; the growth in the group's reputation across Southeast Asia is remarkable. Royalty have visited them. The Vocational School for the Disabled won two gold and one silver medal last year, at the paraplegic Olympic Games in Sydney. This fact alone has brought to the government's attention, the plight of the disabled. Respect for Catholicism and its charitable work is being earned.

There are conversions, a thousand plus now, in and around Pattaya so far, forty from the five establishments. One of these is currently in a seminary, training to be a priest; two others are at university, one training to be a doctor. It is an oasis of Catholicism in a Buddhist country, located in an environment of temptation. Pattaya has an unfortunate reputation among tourists, 'Man's Heaven'! But the five establishments are a beacon of hope for those who were hopeless. Yes, I would say, it is slowly succeeding.

But what of the children themselves you may well ask? Well, one boy left his uniform behind when he went missing earlier this year, so did a bicycle; the staff were very sad. But almost two weeks later he returned with his younger brother, who had also lived on the streets of Bangkok, he was on the crossbar of the bike, which now had two flat tyres. He had ridden to Bangkok and back, a round trip of 140 miles! That's what this work really means, providing an un-dreamt of opportunity for their future, a haven of training, faith, caring and love.

There is a prayer that is quite common here, *"Let us bring joy this day to those who are in need; —and draw them and us nearer to you through the help we give them."*

Chris and Thea made the most of the weekend not knowing when they'd next meet. Their friendship had grown substantially since that night in Washington when they'd recognised each other's depth of feeling. They'd reached a point in their relationship where they couldn't see a future without their friendship. If truth were told, they'd fallen in love, but an unspoken agreement did not recognise the fact, they acted like brother and sister.

A quite significant event occurred on Wednesday 19th, when a letter arrived for Chris from Manny.

Dear Chris,

This is a very belated thank you for the beautiful presentation folder containing your kind note of thanks and your article on 'Creation'. I certainly didn't do very much to help. I purposely left it until now to write, as I didn't want to disturb you at university with what I want to ask.

I'll start with the fact that I've found three more references in the bible, to support the idea of a soul (*spirit* not *breath*) being given to humankind—thus creating mankind.

The most important is from Judges, (I think, sorry, but I've lost my note of the reference). *You spoke, they were made. You sent forth your spirit and it formed them.* Two distinct steps, once again.

From Psalm 104:30. *"But when you sent out your spirit, they were created."* By implication it was a second step that created mankind.

Finally from the prophet Ezekiel: 36: 27. *"I will put my spirit in you and I will see to it that you follow my laws and keep all the commands I have given you."* A statement reinforcing the fact that God put a spirit in mankind—that he gave his commandments to Moses as guidance and possibly the fact that He was to send Christ to show the way mankind should follow?

Now for the real purpose of this letter. I've thought about it a great deal, I want to suggest we write a book based upon your outline, a co-authorship. I've often fancied the idea of writing a book, your 'Creation' is the inspiration I needed. So far as I'm aware, there is no book that sets out to reconcile Charles Darwin's '*The Origin of Species by Means of Natural Selection*' with the Biblical record of creation. Your summary of your conclusions does that and more.

If you are in agreement with this idea, I suggest you write chapter one i.e. the first step of time, and I would write the rest. You know far better than I, what you're talking about in that first part, but I would suggest, with my background, I'm better placed to do the rest.

I think such a book would have appeal as an original work and probably be controversial on at least three issues:

- A reasoned reconciliation of basic biblical events, with the findings of science. It introduces a revolutionary concept—a clear distinction between the *evolution of humankind* and the subsequent *creation of Mankind*. There could be quite a debate?

- It would launch your idea on the revised time span of creation to a much wider public (assuming you are successful with your thesis). The reinterpretation of 'The Hubble Constant' could be another keen debate.

- I suggest we limit the book to the twenty steps of time, as does your document (and I think we should). The steps of time to that point will imply a countdown to the end of the world, just less than two thousand years hence, without actually saying so—an even bigger debate.

There's another reason for my book suggestion; there was a hidden purpose behind your visit to Stonehenge and what happened there. Look at where it's led you, it surely wasn't just to enlighten your family and mine.

There's no hurry, nothing to disturb your studies; I wouldn't want to distract you. It would take me at least a year to eighteen months, so, for example, you might choose to draft the first chapter as next year's summer holiday project? You could even come over here for a couple of weeks, so we could tie things up together. I'm also sure that by then Thea will be dying to see you!

I end with a piece of potentially good news. One can see why you were led to assume that all of humankind must have been created as mankind in 3962 BC, not just Adam & Eve. But a recent article in *Nature* leads one to the possible conclusion that the bible *is* correct. Adam & Eve were the first and only ones created as mankind and all of us come from that beginning. In summary, it says:

"Using a computer model, researchers at MIT (local again!) attempted to trace back our ancestry, through common DNA markers, using estimated patterns of migration throughout history. They concluded that we are all from a common ancestor, who lived in eastern Asia, around 1,415 BC."

They go on to say they found a time when a large fraction of people (mankind?) had developed—while the rest (humankind?) were ancestors of no one alive today; that was around 5,353 BC. Dr Steve Olsen, who led the research, stressed that the dates were estimates.

It doesn't make much sense at the moment, but raises a question for when such DNA research becomes more sophisticated, and backtracking computer programmes more accurate. It might well be that the 1,415 BC date eventually becomes 3,926 BC, and the stock of humankind sinks to zero thereafter?

I've gone on long enough, probably too long, but please think about what I suggest. Perhaps you will let me know before you return to Cambridge in the New Year?

Tell Thea I love her and look forward to her return in a few days. You and your family have my very best wishes for Christmas and the New Year.

My regards,
Manny.

Pat and Eugene broke up from school for the Christmas holiday at midday on Wednesday 20th. Thea, having been made aware of this date previously, had booked to take the afternoon flight BA 215, rather than the morning flight, to allow her to spend a little more time with them.

Pat had prepared a typical Christmas dinner for that evening, which they all thoroughly enjoyed, albeit Helen's absence dampened the event a little. They pulled crackers and exchanged presents, drinking and chatting quite late into the night. They were fairly late up the following morning, Chris and Thea going for a short walk to blow the cobwebs away before a light lunch.

Pat and Gene having said their goodbyes, Chris took Thea to Heathrow for her 4 o'clock flight to Boston. The check-in queue was not bad, she hadn't got too much baggage as she'd taken some of her things back when she went home for the Thanksgiving weekend in November. They had a final coffee together, and as they embraced before she disappeared through passport control, Thea whispered in his ear, "Look under your bed when you get back Chris, Father Christmas brought an early surprise."

As soon as Christopher got home, he went to his room and found a book under his bed, *Charles Kingsley and His Ideas,* By G. Kendall, published in 1947. Inside Thea had written,

He took it downstairs to show his mother in particular; she was impressed, not only by the thought, but also by the fact that Thea must have hunted high and low to find a copy.

Thea landed in Boston, five minutes early, at 6:30 local time, that evening. Her father was there to meet her, as she came from the customs hall with her cases on a trolley, they saw each other and embraced. She was pleased to be home once again, no more flying around and living out of suitcases for quite a while, she hoped. When they got home, she and her father spent a very pleasant evening in each other's company, talking about their jobs, the plans he'd made for Christmas, and of course Chris.

Manny wanted to know how Chris had reacted to his letter, she thought favourably, but said he would write early in the New Year. She thought he was exhibiting some signs of single-mindedness, a determination to master his subjects and ultimately his thesis, but not quite to the exclusion of all else.

When she went to bed she opened her case to get out her overnight things, only to find a beautiful eternity ring with a note. He must have put it there when he had gone to bring her case down to the car. The note read, 'For a friend I value above all others—Happy Christmas'. She then realised how he really felt; his preoccupation and slight coolness were probably his way of handling their current relationship. He didn't want to get too emotionally involved while he concentrated on his studies. His feelings obviously ran somewhat deeper than appeared to be the case. She decided to keep the ring in her bedside draw, perhaps sharing his feeling that theirs was a secret love for the present.

Chris spent much of his holiday doing research at Maidenhead library. During the previous term, when he needed a break, he had researched the world's raw materials and world energy supplies. Now he was concerned with learning as much as possible about Hubble the astronomer and the environment. In the latter case this became four subjects—meteorology, the ocean currents, the 'greenhouse effect' and volcanism.

He wrote to Manny before he returned to Cambridge, agreeing in principle to what he proposed. He would only want to proceed however, if and when his thesis was accepted. If Manny were happy to start drafting the book on that basis, he would be happy to review the whole project in the summer.

When he returned to Cambridge he dedicated himself once more to learning all he could from his tutors. From his questioning he extracted more and more of their knowledge and experience. As he constantly reviewed Macuzio's notes he began occasionally to get the odd glimmer of light. He began to see glimpses—nuances within the math and physics concepts that might have led Macuzio slightly astray. As the term progressed he became somewhat surer that he could begin to see a way to balance the equations; a way to break out of the deadlock that had stopped Macuzio making further progress.

He didn't let himself get too excited, for he could only catch a glimpse as if through a mist, but it helped to give his solitary task a lot of encouragement.

One significant distraction did occur quite early in the term, a letter from his sister Helen. It read:

Dear Mum, Dad and Chris,

It was nice to chat on the phone with each of you on Christmas Day, it made me quite home sick and I shed a few tears afterwards. But the work here is worth it—it feels so rewarding. Although it's a Buddhist country, here in the orphanage we celebrated Christmas, as Christians, for obvious reasons. In the end I went to three parties, one in the orphanage where I work, one with the old people and one with the street kids.

The magic of Christmas morning was the present giving accompanied by the bells of Christmas. I will never forget the joy of seeing the tiny ones coming up to receive a package of Christmas gifts from Fr. Brennan, sometimes bigger than they themselves. One could see in their faces the sheer excitement of not knowing what was in the package, but knowing that whatever it was it would be wonderful.

In my earlier letter you may remember there are two elder boys who are away at university, they were able to come back for Christmas Day. At the end of the present giving one went up to Fr. Brennan and gave him a model of a church he'd made. As he gave it to Fr. Brennan he said it was a gift from his heart for all the help he had given him. He grasped Fr. Brennan's hands, and kissed them, then they hugged and Fr. Brennan told him he loved him, which brought tears to all our eyes! I didn't hear clearly what was said in Thai, but I was able to clarify it later when I had a chat to the 'boy'. His English is quite good and my Thai continues to improve.

His nickname is 'Tong', his proper name is Ton Kae-Kang-Pu. He's twenty, will be twenty-one in May and he's the one studying medicine in Bangkok. He came to the orphanage in 1989 at the age of eight when his mother died of

AIDS. Before being accepted he had a complete medical check-up and was found to be completely free of the infection.

This brings me to the primary purpose of this letter, it's addressed specifically to mum and dad, but of course I've sent a copy to Chris. I haven't spoken to you on the phone about what I've been thinking, for two reasons. I've only just made up my mind and it is probably better to put my thoughts in writing to you first anyway.

When I was speaking to Tong on Christmas Day he told me he had asked Fr. Brennan if he could become a Catholic, when he came back to the orphanage for the long holiday, which is early in the year here. Fr. Brennan has now organised a programme of instruction for him, with the help of two of the nuns. I've asked if I might join him with a view to considering such a change for myself? Fr. Brennan said I was welcome to join him.

I hope it doesn't come as a complete surprise: I am mindful of the talks we've had at home. We've discussed the fact that that the Anglican Church had become very divided over the issue of female priests and many of its clergy had, or were considering, becoming Catholics as a result. We'd also discussed the much more damaging acceptance of homosexual marriage and even the possibility of homosexual clergy. These two facts, along with my experience here, have caused me to question my remaining an Anglican; these events have unsettled me spiritually. I cannot see that a church so vehemently divided within, can survive in the longer term.

You are by now well aware of what is being done here by Catholics in Thailand, and I have come to think that Catholicism could be my true spiritual home.

I know its dogma is much more dogmatic, but as such it offers one a firmer foundation to one's faith. I see joining Tong, on the programme of instruction, as a step in helping me to finally make up my mind, I do hope you understand. I have not made the final decision and no doubt when we next speak on the phone, I will get your reaction to all of this?

I hope and pray for your understanding.

Much love,
Helen.

Chapter Ten
Graduate

The main topic of conversation when Christopher first came home for the Easter Holiday was Helen. Her six months of voluntary work was due to end in a few days on 31st March, which happened to be Easter Sunday. She had decided to convert to Catholicism and this would happen on Easter Saturday evening during the vigil mass.

It seemed that she and Tong had become close friends during the Thai holiday. Being funded by the orphanage through his medical studies, he spent his holiday giving something back by painting and decorating. Moving around the same premises, undergoing religious instruction together and having a shared interest in medicine, they were naturally drawn together. While they both worked during the day, they began seeing each other most evenings, each to practice the other's language initially.

Now she had decided to stay an extra week to have a week's holiday with Tong before he returned to university. They were going off on the Monday after the Easter celebrations. She would now be coming home overnight on a Qantas flight, arriving at Heathrow on Tuesday 9th April.

The discussion about Helen led him and his parents on his second evening at home, to talk once again about religion and the state of the Anglican Church. Pat and Gene in particular had been troubled by the introduction of women priests, they could not give a sound reason, it just felt wrong. They thought it had arisen from the growing momentum behind equal rights for women, it seemed to them like an ecclesiastical whim, to be seen to give women equal opportunity.

On the other hand, all three were very clear regarding homosexuality. They recognised that while there were people made that way, they felt that some might have decided to be deviant, due to a bad experience with women, but most, in their view, practiced it for the thrill of 'illicit' sex. Everyone is tempted, each in different ways, genuine homosexuals should be given understanding and tolerance, but like all sin, it was to be fought against.

Pat in particular could not understand how practicing clergy, not only condoned such behaviour, but also in some cases, indulge in such practices themselves. All three felt that it had been sanctioned as a result of the human rights legislation gone mad. The law gave them the right to be homosexuals, but it blinded them to what the bible has to say.

Pat said, "How could they ignore the biblical story that brought the destruction of Sodom, whose men were homosexuals." She quoted, *they called out to Lot and asked, "Where are the men who came to stay with you tonight? Bring them out to us! The men of Sodom want to have sex with them." Lot went outside and closed the door behind him. He said to them, "Friends, I beg you, don't do such a wicked thing!"*

These clergy choose to forget the bible they preach, when it suits them. In Leviticus it says quite clearly and unequivocally, '*No man is to have sexual relations with another man; God hates that*'.

In Helen's case, the earlier family discussions had finally led to her decision. The Anglican position was slowly deteriorating; a schism might well be the final outcome. The Anglican condition, and Helen's decision, had somehow precipitated the needed to make their own decision, individually or collectively.

Gene made a suggestion. "Unfortunately we won't be there to see Helen enter the Catholic church. Let me phone the priest at St Joseph's to enquire about the time of the vigil mass on Saturday, also, if anyone's entering the church here in Maidenhead. Perhaps we can all go and see Helen's decision being put into practice locally? Chris has been there with Thea of course, but it might help us with our own decision."

They went on Saturday evening, there were three adult converts, one who had not been baptised. It was one of the longest services of the liturgical year, but full of joy and hope for the future. They were glad they went, not only to share Helen's experience, but also to pray for their own guidance.

They all went to Heathrow to meet Helen, as they hugged and kissed they noticed how brown she was. Within a day it was clear that whereas a senior school sixth former had left last September, an assured, quite mature young lady had arrived back home. She was full of stories of her travels in Thailand from her holidays, Pattaya and the five different homes/schools, and how she missed the young babies. She explained a little how the Thai language mainly consisted of small words, for example the babies up to kindergarten age, one to four, were sub-divided as—little littles, big littles, little bigs and big bigs! She talked a lot about Tong and it was clear she had a very soft spot for him. She looked up to him as he was already in his second year of medical studies.

She had decided she would now offer her services to the Pattaya Orphanage Trust in London. It would be on a temporary basis for three or four days a week while mum and dad were back at school and Chris back in Cambridge. This would be up to the summer holidays, which she'd planned to spend at home with them, until she went off to her medical studies at Imperial College in the autumn.

Chris and Helen discovered how much they'd missed each other. They caught up with each other by spending time together, occasionally going to the cinema, swimming, indoor bowling or driving into the countryside for long walks. They talked a great deal about Tong and Thea, it was clear to each; that the other had probably met the person they would ultimately marry.

During their walks they talked on many topics. They talked about Helen's decision to become a Catholic and Chris mentioned the influence the events surrounding the document had had on his spiritual outlook. The Easter Vigil mass at St Joseph's, the fact that Thea was a Catholic and the state of the Anglican Church had made up his mind to convert. He felt that the Anglican Church was allowing baser human instincts to have an ever-increasing influence, to the detriment of the church's spiritual outlook. He would not be surprised if it were weakened still further, splitting into two or more sub-churches, with ever decreasing moral authority. He asked if she would enquire of the priest at St Joseph's how he might do what she'd done.

They discussed his studies at Cambridge and how the Macuzio meeting had given him renewed impetus and commitment. He had kept in touch with him and debated his evolving ideas with him via email. They talked of her forthcoming four years of medical studies and whether her friendship with Tong would in fact survive such an extended period of separation. She told Chris that she had in mind to pay for Tong to come to England when he qualified. It would be a holiday in which they could see if they still felt the same about each other and meet the family. She confided in him that her daydream was to persuade Tong to go into the medical practice in Pattaya that also looked after the needs of the children in the various schools and homes. In her unspoken plan she hoped she would be able to join the practice when she qualified two years after him.

Chris mentioned that he had been doing some background research into the ten decrees, the topics listed in the document. He asked Helen if she would write some notes for him, on how she saw the future of medicine evolving.

Helen also spent time with mum and dad. During that time Chris would go to the Maidenhead Reference Library to do more background research. His possible post-graduate studies were never too far from his mind, along with his determination to produce a unique doctoral thesis.

On his return to Cambridge, Chris became single-minded once again, determined to obtain a double first. In the process he was able to make further headway with the initial speed of expansion from the 'Big Bang', this could also have an effect on the speed of light?

During the term, as he became more familiar with abstruse aspects of physics and maths, he had his first breakthrough.

He felt sure he had finally resolved the logic problem of how the Macuzio equations related to Einstein's theory of relativity. He was able to create a balance, within the mathematical equations, when he applied an initial escape velocity for the 'Big Bang' of 598,920 miles per second, or 3.22 times the present speed of light! Only a week or so later, Macuzio emailed his congratulations. Chris now felt that his dreamed-of thesis had at last become a real possibility.

Encouraged by his success, he concentrated on his studies and final exams, for the remainder of the term. He even 'forgot' any further research work on the document for the time being. He never forgot Thea though, he kept in regular touch by email and phone.

His parents and Helen came to Cambridge for the graduation ceremony. They were proud to learn he had obtained a double first in Physics and Mathematics. Over tea and biscuits they were told his marks were among the highest ever achieved. He was invited to stay on for a year's post-graduate studies with a view to obtaining a doctorate in cosmology.

On his return home for the summer holiday he began to relax for the first time in almost a year; he realised just how much he'd missed Thea. He'd already arranged to go over to Boston for three weeks in July, when Thea and Manny had arranged their summer holiday. He needed to discuss and finalise Manny's wish to publish a book, but more importantly he needed to see and be with Thea, he hadn't seen her for almost seven months.

His single-minded determination with his studies, his simultaneous preoccupation with the Macuzio conundrum, and his occasional research into the decree aspects of the document for relaxation, had all caused him to submerge his feelings for Thea. He now realised, and was prepared to recognise for the first time; he was in love with her. He thought it must have been a subconscious development, for now it welled up in him with a force that was hard to control. He had two weeks to wait before he went to Boston. He also recalled the promise he'd made to his mother and decided to make an early opportunity to speak with her alone.

His parents had two more days before their schools broke up for the holidays and Helen was due to finish working for the Pattaya Orphanage Trust at the end of the week. Christopher had decided to go ahead with the book idea, subject to what Manny proposed and had drafted.

For his part he began to elaborate on what he had written almost a year ago. He could incorporate his vision, without indicating its source, and he could enlarge on Charles Kingsley's ideas following what he had learnt from the book Thea gave him for Christmas. He liked the latter point, because it painted a clearer picture of the immensity of God's intellect, in deciding and implementing all the details of his creation in a few moments of time. Added to this he could now enhance the description of the process, that by which the universe made itself. He had now developed a mental picture that would be the main thrust of his thesis; this provided a much clearer understanding of God's brilliance in creating the conditions for the making, of what for us, is a very complex universe.

A few days later he was at something of a loose end and offered to help his mother clear the lunch table and put the crockery in the dishwasher. Eugene retired to the study to catch up with correspondence and bills he'd left until the holiday and Helen, who had been primed by Chris, said she was going to her room to write to Tong.

Chris made coffee for everyone and after taking it to his father and to Helen, he and his mother took theirs into the garden. He explained to his mother that it was as if he had surfaced once more into the real world. What with his preoccupation with the document last summer and then a very single-minded approach to his studies for the last year, he realised he had been detached, in another world. Now he had his degrees and a clear idea of the direction he wanted to take with his post-graduate studies he was really relaxing for the first time in quite a while.

Pat recognised he wanted to tell her something, but didn't know how to begin, so she said, "It's Thea you really want to talk about isn't it Chris?"

"Yes mum, it is. I've come to realise more and more, ever since the degree ceremony really, that I'm in love with her. I just can't wait to go to Boston and see her. We've stayed in touch as you know and for this last year she's been a very good friend, but now I realise that deep down I've loved her for quite a while. I promised I'd let you know if my feelings changed, they have, and in a couple of weeks I'll find out if Thea feels the same."

"Chris, I'm so pleased you told me. I think you'll find she feels the same way. Your father and I discussed it after Thea came for the weekend. We liked her very much, and even then thought she was in love with you. As you said, you were preoccupied, otherwise you'd have seen it yourself. I'm not pushing the idea at all, but you're twenty-three and she's twenty-five; see how you feel after your holiday in Boston, she'd be a good wife. I'll tell your father what we've discussed, but otherwise it's just between us until you say otherwise."

"I love you mum, and thanks for taking it so calmly."

"I love you too Chris, I've seen it coming for a year now, it's something that had to come with both you and Helen; I wonder what Tong's like?"

"Mum, while I've got you on your own, I'd like to ask another favour. I've been doing bits of research into the ten decrees listed in the document. I've asked grandpa to write me some notes on farming; I've asked Helen to do the same on the future of medicine as she sees it; can I ask you to address the decree that says *make final call to conversion?*

"There's no rush, as you know Thea's father wants to write a joint authorship book, based on my outline. If we agree, when I'm over there, I'll probably have to write my part when I get back. I still want to finish my understanding of the whole document though, when I can."

"I'll do that for you, Chris. I'll need to think about it for a bit; I'll try and make a start this holiday if I can."

"Thanks mum, your great, thanks a lot."

Chris and Helen again spent some time together, not as intensely as during the Easter holidays, but because he would be gone for three weeks of this holiday. She told him she had thought about the notes he wanted on the future of medicine. She'd already started doing some research on her days off, realising that making such notes for him, would be a good preparation for her start at Imperial College, she was going to continue to do this as her holiday project.

Helen took Chris to Heathrow for the 10:40 BA flight to Boston. Knowing how Thea felt about Chris, Manny told her to meet him on her own. She got to Logan Airport by 12:30

just in case the flight was early. As she waited she could hardly contain herself. The way she felt, the seven moths separation had been a very long time indeed, made more so by having to ensure Chris was not distracted from his studies. In the event the flight was ten minutes late, landing at 1:45 local time.

When he emerged from the customs and immigration hall, he dropped his suitcase as soon as he saw Thea and took her in his arms, kissing her affectionately. Breaking apart he said "I've missed you so much, it's made me realise just how much I love you."

"Oh Chris, I've loved you from the moment I first saw you, I felt sure that one day you'd feel the same."

"Let's go and have a coffee before you drive me home, so I can take a good look at you and see what I've been missing."

Manny was very pleased to see Christopher, and during the afternoon all three caught up on the details of life. Manny and Thea repeated their congratulations on his double first; Manny adding that he hadn't doubted that result for a minute, Thea saying how sorry she was that she could not be there with his family for the graduation ceremony.

Thea had now settled into her job at MIT, got to know some of the staff and made them all laugh when she talked of some of their mannerisms, foibles and eccentricities.

Manny said he was pleased with the progress he'd made on the book and suggested the best approach might be for Christopher to read the draft manuscript, as far as it was written, notes and all. Then they could discuss if and how they might proceed? Chris said he would enjoy that and suggested that he read it when he was fresh in the morning, as he would probably wake early.

When Thea had gone from the room to prepare an evening meal, Chris asked Manny if he had any objections to him asking Thea to marry him? Manny was surprised at the unexpected question, somewhat unusual in this day and age, although he had seen signs that they'd grown closer.

"No, Chris, quite the reverse. She hasn't spoken about it, but I know she loves you and you'll make a fine pair."

"I haven't spoken to her about it yet, but I thought we might go to New York for two or three days in the middle week of my stay, I'll ask her then."

"That sounds like a good idea, it'll give us time to discuss the book before you go and settle any afterthoughts when you're back."

"What are you two talking about in my absence?" Thea said, as she came back into the room, "You look a little guilty."

"I was asking Manny if he had any objections to my taking you to New York for two or three days in the middle week of my stay."

"Oh Chris, that sounds wonderful, I haven't been there in quite a while, and there's plenty to see and do. Maybe we'd need three or four days as you've never been. It's a great idea; I'll make some bookings tomorrow while you two discuss your book."

Chris started on Manny's manuscript quite early the following morning and learnt a great deal in the process. First and foremost was the realisation that his original write-up of Creation did not contain its sources, references, observations or proofs to support the text. Manny had recognised the need to explain each step so the pages were sub-divided. An explanation of what had occurred, with appropriate symbols for references, proofs and the logic of the conclusions, on the lower part of the appropriate page.

Then, for example, on the third day of creation and beyond, when the land masses had appeared and were moving over time, he had confused the various names and locations. Additionally he had totally missed that part of Pangea called Oceania; this eventually broke away from Antarctica to form what are now Australia and New Zealand.

As he read on, he liked Manny's style and also noticed that Manny was less dogmatic about the causes that brought changes to the path of evolution. For example, the asteroid impact in Mexico at Chicxulub during day six might have had a number of consequences, any or all of which might have occurred. The supersonic shock wave, a tsunami up to 1,000 feet high that washed over great swathes of land, a shaking of the earth's crust that caused a spate of volcanoes, a darkening of the skies due to the huge amount of dust and debris thrown up, etc. In other words, where Manny was not sure, and a number of competing explanations had not yet been resolved, he gave room to them all.

The latter part of Manny's writing was still in note form; again Chris saw that many additional factors had been added. Manny had mentioned to him about the DNA backwardation that might show that Adam & Eve, were in fact, the first of all mankind. Manny now came across more references where evidence showed that two or more forms of Homo Erectus and/or Homo Sapiens continued to live for some considerable time alongside mankind, before dying out. He quoted Dr Gee, a senior editor of the journal *Nature,* who apparently said, "It is a remarkable fact that it is only at this moment in seven million years that there is one species of human on the planet." Manny modified this to read, "One species of mankind!"

Later in the day Chris and Manny became immersed in a discussion about the book. Christopher said how much he liked Manny's approach to the nature of the book and his style of writing. They agreed that each of the first five days of creation would be a chapter, sub-divided into three parts, flora, fauna and geography. Day six would be divided into the fifteen steps of time—the steps of humankind's evolution and finally mankind's creation.

They agreed that there should be no mention of the document; it would raise more questions than it answered. This left the problem of how to arrive at the steps of time—a rationale was needed. Chris said he'd thought about this and proposed he dealt with it in a foreword; this he would draft while he was here, to set the tone for further discussion between them. He went on to suggest that he'd also write a prologue, on his return to England, based on an expansion of what he'd said about the works of Charles Kingsley. Manny was pleased with both suggestions and readily agreed. Discussions continued for the first week, immersed in ever more detail, but broken up by enjoyable excursions; time spent going out and about with Thea and sometimes with her father as well.

Chris and Thea flew down to New York the following Monday and stayed at the Hilton hotel in Manhattan. They found a lovely small restaurant for their evening meal; after dining as well as if they were in the George V in Brussels, Christopher asked Thea to marry him. She said yes without hesitation, so the following day they spent a considerable time looking for the right engagement ring. They finally settled on a one and a half carat diamond solitaire; they also bought a pair of wedding rings.

The next three days went in something of a whirl. They talked about their finances, where they would get married and when, where they would live, their work plans, and a thousand details. This was between visits to the theatre, the Russian Tea Rooms, a concert in Carnegie Hall, Times Square, the top of the Empire State building and the Statue of Liberty. They also went to say a prayer at Ground Zero. They flew back to Boston on Thursday evening, tired but very happy. Manny was delighted with their news.

Most of Friday was spent in conversation with Manny and, via the phone, with Chris's parents, discussing their outline plans. By the end of the day there was general agreement. Chris would go back for a brief visit to Boston over Thanksgiving weekend in November. Manny and Thea would go to England for Christmas, and subject to his grandparents' agreement to accommodate him, Manny would stay over for the New Year as well. Thea would then visit England for two weeks at Easter, to discuss and make wedding arrangements with Chris's mother and to look at houses around Cambridge with Chris. She'd leave her job at the end of May to go back to England for the wedding on the 21st June—midsummer's day.

Chris spent most of Saturday writing the foreword to the book. He wanted to keep it as near to the truth as possible. He also needed to set the right tone for the book and after numerous false starts, trying to find the right words, he eventually managed to say what he wanted on a single page.

Foreword

When I was compiling my PhD thesis, I had calculated a radically reduced age of the universe—this figure was still huge and turned out to be 8,220,835,840 years ago—effectively the starting point of this book.

I'd always loved playing with numbers and at one time I'd established the number of years that had elapsed from Adam & Eve to the birth of Christ. I did this from the ages of each generation, as given in Genesis and the c. 1900-year historical context of the period between Abraham to Christ. It totalled 3,920 years. This aroused my curiosity, as it was almost one thousandth of the 3.4 million years that humans have been on Earth?

As a younger man, my father had given me a book called 'Future Shock'; some of you may have read it? I was intrigued by Alvin Toffler's portrayal of the way life on Earth was speeding up.

I was idly playing with the age of the universe number on another occasion, thought of Toffler's concept, and decided to continually halve the age of the universe. It was a vague thought about the half-life of time, rather than the half-life of atomic radiation. Imagine my surprise when I came to 3,920 at the twenty-first halving. This equates to 3,926 BC, the creation of Adam & Eve, because Christ was born in 6 BC!

This time my curiosity was aroused to the point of taking action, so I set about trying to solve the apparent dichotomy with the help of friends—this book is the result.

My co-author and I became intrigued with the quest for ever more answers as the research unfolded. When we'd finished, an obvious title sprang to mind—*Twenty-One Steps of Time.*

When he gave it to Manny to read he said, "I've written it as an act of faith, that my thesis will actually come to this predetermined conclusion, heaven knows what we'll do if I'm wrong?"

"You were driven to arrive at that figure, I too have faith, and it's fine by me."

Chris spent a great deal of time with Thea during his third week, and progressively less with Manny, as the book details to be settled diminished. When he finally left to return to England it was quite a wrench, there were tears, but they were secure in their love for each other. They had made their plans, had a real sense of purpose and much to look forward to, Thanksgiving weekend was not too far away.

Once back in England the first couple of days were spent discussing all that had happened, with his parents and Helen. It wasn't just his engagement and all that flowed from it, but also the progress made with Manny over the forthcoming book.

Helen had made the enquiries he'd requested about religious instruction; the result was the name of a Catholic priest and Parish in Cambridge. If he contacted him on his return to Cambridge in September, he could join a programme, common to the church in this country, with a view to becoming a Catholic at Easter. She had told mum and dad about it in his absence and they'd decided that they would do the same thing at St Joseph's; they would all be able to enter together.

He was spending much of his remaining holiday, writing a preface, and an expanded version of his earlier presentation folder. They cautioned him to keep it in layman's language and not get carried away with the science. In fact he'd brought a photocopy of Manny's writing to help him to emulate the style as far as possible.

When he started on the preface, he decided to use the words spoken in his vision. As his memory of it got more distant, so did his incredulity that it had ever happened. He didn't mention his vision for obvious reasons; he would simply let the reader think it was a piece of fiction to set the scene for the book's content. He did strongly acknowledge the work of Charles Kingsley in portraying the kind of universe that God created and why.

In writing chapter one he kept largely to an expanded version of what he'd previously written. The major difference was the addition of a glossary on almost every page. It offered explanations of the more abstruse words, references to the bible passages and scientific papers that had been written on the formation of the universe.

When he'd finished, he emailed it to Manny, asking him to offer a critique and to add references in the blank spaces in the references relating to the Earth's early formation.

Manny hadn't let on about his sadness at the thought that Thea would end up so far away, he hadn't wanted to dampen their spirits. He thought he might sound out friends and colleagues about the prospect of getting a museum job in London. His spirits lifted at the idea that he might visit one or two of them during the Christmas—New Year holiday? There were no family ties to keep him in America and he'd got a good reputation in his field and a wealth of experience to offer.

He'd still got her at home for another year while he'd be busy finishing the book. He'd got time to make up his mind and his Christmas visit to England could well help. It might be that Chris, with his qualifications, could decide to get a good job in America, who knows?

Chapter Eleven
Thesis

Christopher's mathematical ability had shown itself from quite an early age. The concept of numbers, two and three dimensional geometry and the logic of algebra, had all come easily to him. By fourteen his father had taught him calculus, logarithms and trigonometry. This, in turn enabled him to read and understand Max Born's book on Einstein's theory—Special Relativity, by the time he went to university.

He struggled with Einstein's book of 1921, The Meaning of Relativity, dealing with his General Theory. It later transpired there were two reasons for this. First, that Einstein's maths was non-standard, he used his own symbols for many concepts, secondly, it was only in his first year at Cambridge that Christopher mastered the more difficult concept of differential geometry, enabling him to study and understand the General Theory.

During his second year he'd learnt that Einstein had made a significant error in his maths that made him conceive the idea of a static universe. This became known as the 'Steady State' theory within which he created a concept called a 'cosmological constant' to solve the problems associated with it. A Russian named Friedmann detected Einstein's error in

1922, predicting that Einstein's theory led to an expanding, not static, universe. Einstein eventually conceded the point, for in the late 1920's, Hubble's observations showed that the universe was indeed expanding, galaxies are moving away from each other and the further away they are, the faster the speed—now known as Hubble's Law.

It was at this point in Christopher's education, just a few weeks before the end of his second year at Cambridge, that he experienced the strange events at Stonehenge. This had led to his summer of wrestling with the validity of the document he'd discovered. It also introduced him to the topic of VSL (Variable Speed of Light) through the excitement of meeting Dr Macuzio in America.

His subsequent detailed questioning of masters, fellows and dons, which began very early in his third year, led him to learn much more about early VSL theory. This wasn't a theory about light *per se,* it just happens to be the visible part of the spectrum referred to as electro-magnetic radiation. VSL was not taught—the 'heresy' was in its infancy, it was only spoken about as the direct result of his questions, and then in the equivalent of hushed voices. His tutors were of the opinion that no respectable cosmologist would put his 'head above the parapet' by publishing a paper. That would be seen as questioning Einstein's theory of relativity, that brilliant advance in understanding cosmology. A major plank of Einstein's theory is the absolute value of the speed of light; it is a cornerstone of his work. He had shown that nothing in the universe can travel faster than electro-magnetic radiation, which has a speed of 186,322.27 miles per second in a vacuum—that is six hundred and seventy million, seven hundred and sixty thousand, one hundred and sixty miles per hour!

Dr Macuzio had reason to think that the speed of light must have been exceeded in the very early stages of the Big Bang? Other cosmologists had slowly emerged to raise similar questions; admitting there might be cases where this speed could be exceeded under certain circumstances? Others chose to develop concepts that circumvented the problem with other ideas. Albrecht, for example had introduced the idea of 'Inflation' in the universe. This topic, and other speculative conjectures had only been picked up and openly talked about by 'rash' cosmologists, since about 1997.

One can just imagine Christopher's excitement that here, at the very forefront of cosmological thinking and debate, was the idea he'd had on the train back from Brussels, during his summer holidays. His was not based upon cosmological thinking, but the need to solve a steps of time problem associated with the document. His fortuitous meeting with Dr Macuzio had, in effect, thrown him in at the deep end of VSL theory. Whereas he'd had an open mind on pursuing string theory, quantum physics or cosmology as a post-graduate, he was now hooked on the latter.

His continued questioning of his tutors during his third year, exposed him to many differing ideas. The horizon problem—if the speed of light was forever constant? There was the flatness problem, yet space was curved, which led him into an understanding of Bianchi Identities. There were many variations of inflation theory put forward; however none entirely solved the problem. Perhaps the greatest of these was proposed by Alan Guth where the Big Bang was so hot he likened it to 'Liquid Lava'.

He entered the realms of quantum physics and what was called the Planck Epoch—that infinitesimal fraction of a second that was the start of the Big Bang, which no one had yet figured out. He became embroiled in Kaluza—Klein's 'String Theory' and the concepts of multi-dimensional space.

He wrestled with cosmological perturbation theory and the associated massive algebraic calculations. He learnt about Lorentz Transformations and a thing called an 'Atomic Fine Structure Constant', discussed by John Barrow. This affects the way electrons absorb discrete and minute fractions of the light spectrum when passing through a gas cloud. This effect changes if the speed of light differs from the norm.

He started to use the cosmological web site where many papers had begun to appear in preference to specialist magazine publishing. This enabled him to do his own research into VSL concepts. He read papers by Moffat and Clayton, papers on the 'horizon' of Black Holes, M-theory and Branes, and papers by Kiritsis and Stephon. As he probed deeper and deeper, he was exposed to non-communicative geometry and quantum gravity, a paper by Lee and the Portuguese cosmologist, Magueijo.

He had come a very long way, both in his education and his cosmological thinking, by sheer hard work. By the time he sat his finals—the summer break was welcome indeed.

In spite of falling in love, getting engaged to Thea in America and agreeing to a book based on his ideas; he spent a considerable part of his time cogitating the form his PhD thesis should take.

On his return to Cambridge for his post-graduate studies, he had mapped out in his mind the line of his investigations.

His starting point was a statement made by Einstein in 1911, 'gravitation slows down light'.

This was one of the thoughts of the great man, as he considered what became his General Theory in 1915. Christopher wished to investigate this idea as he felt it was 'forgotten' as Einstein latched onto his growing belief in the fixed speed of light. He felt it had been pushed even further away in his thinking as he developed his 'steady state' idea of a static universe.

A second, but parallel line of investigation, was the work done by Friedmann from which he concluded that the universe was expanding. His statement in 1922 that 'the universe expands forever, gradually decelerating, but never quite stopping' was another motivating concept for Christopher.

These two men stood out as pre-eminent thinkers, between them they changed the way of thinking about the universe. If both of their statements were true, then it would seem that the speed of light must have been very considerably higher at the start of the Big Bang. He reasoned that the horizon problem arose due to Hubble's Law, the greater the distance, the ever-increasing speed of expansion. At about 16 billion light years from Earth, this speed was greater than the speed of light, so one could not see objects at any greater distance. Chris felt that logic dictated that if the speed of light could not be exceeded, this particular conclusion was not possible. This was an indication however; those speeds greater than the speed of light must be possible, which was what he now instinctively believed.

This line of thesis development was supported by the observations of Webb and his team in the University of New

South Wales in Sydney, in the late 1990's. The change in the alpha observations, where light from ever more distant galaxies had passed through gas clouds, showed that the speed of light increased with distance. This was fact, potentially another Hubble type law, yet to be fully developed. As the light of these observations took thousands, if not millions of light years to reach us, they were observations of an ever more distant past in the development of the universe. This he felt was the key to his thesis.

He had listed two other lines of investigation he would need to undertake before he could hope to finalise his paper. He needed to understand more clearly the cosmologically accepted way in which energy was transformed into matter due to the tension created in an expanding universe. Also there was some recent theoretical work, which showed that where temperatures are at unbelievably high levels, as was inevitably the case at the start of the Big Bang, the speed of light appeared to increase to an almost infinite degree.

He dug for information, he studied, he wrestled with concepts, he pursued and abandoned blind alleys and he immersed himself in the associated mathematical problems. He would sometimes stay up to one or two in the morning, when the adrenalin was flowing. He nonetheless looked forward to his daily conversations with Thea with great anticipation. He also started his visits to the presbytery, for religious instruction on Thursday evenings. His only sustained break from the intensity of his endeavours was the five-day, long weekend, when he went to Boston for Thanksgiving, a wonderful experience. They both found that absence really does make the heart grow fonder; they had missed each other greatly, it was a magical interlude. Chris was also able to read just over half of Manny's final manuscript for the book; he was greatly impressed.

Thea and Manny came to England for the Christmas— New Year break, as planned. They were made very welcome and had a great time melding easily with the Allen family. Manny enjoyed staying on the farm in Oxfordshire and was particularly pleased to be taken to see Stonehenge, Tate Modern, and the V&A and Science museums. Christopher's grandparents enjoyed having him; they particularly enjoyed his stories with their deep sense of early history. During their conversations at the farm, Manny mentioned his secret concern at being isolated in America, once Thea was married. He said he was considering whether to apply for a museum position in England and planned to start making enquiries in the New Year. They suggested, that if it looked promising, he was welcome to fix interviews for June/July. To that end he could stay with them for a month, if he wished, when he came over for the wedding. He was extremely grateful for their kind offer.

On his return after Christmas, Chris knuckled down to begin to construct a mathematically validated outline of his thesis. He had constantly returned to the datum of known facts and observed phenomena. He abandoned many of the interesting avenues he'd explored, as speculation of the 'what if' variety. While these were a valid means of attempting to hit upon a truth, they had no basis in fact, other than a mathematical consequence of the 'what if' question. Einstein and Friedmann's ideas, along with a couple of 'what if's' that fitted his own ideas, were the exception.

By the time of the Easter break he had become sure that he would make a valid contribution to the VSL question.

In early March, before the Easter break at the end of the month, he'd contacted a few estate agents for details of new housing being built around Cambridge. They proved keen to show them to him and Thea when she came; it was not often that a first-time buyer appeared that could offer a 50% deposit. They finally settled on a new, three-bedroom detached house which was virtually complete, in a nice suburb of the city. The early July availability also coincided with their anticipated return from honeymoon; they would then have the fun of furnishing it together.

On Easter Saturday evening they all went to St Joseph's for the Vigil Service of Light. Thea was delighted to sponsor Chris's entry into the Catholic church, Helen was proud to be her father's sponsor and a long-time Catholic friend of Pat's, from her university days, sponsored her. After the service, they all went back to the Allen house, spiritually uplifted, for a late celebratory supper which went on past midnight.

Thea and his mother spent quite a lot of the holiday making all the wedding arrangements, which was now just over two months away. When he and Thea discussed where they would go for their honeymoon, they finally settled on Manny's offer of using his house as a base in the USA, as he'd decided he would stay over in Oxfordshire for three or four weeks. There were some parts of America Thea wanted to see, before settling overseas and Chris, having seen only a little, was pleased at the idea of seeing more.

On his return to Cambridge after the Easter holiday he finalised his thesis. For obvious reasons one can only attempt a layman's description of it. Christopher had eliminated many of the problems previously associated with VSL by reaffirming Einstein's principle that nothing can exceed the speed of light, but that the speed of light was much faster at the beginning of time.

Subconsciously aware of his conversion to Catholicism at Easter, he decided to be bold. No scientist had yet solved the quantum physics of the Planck Epoch, that 0.42 part of a second, the start of the Big Bang. While scorn might be thrown on his non-scientific opening, he boldly stated that God made the universe by means of creating a singularity from nothing.

He followed this by addressing the question of the remaining 0.58 of that first second of time. He did not know what the speed of light was during that moment, what he did know was that it was in excess of 3.22 times the current speed of light. He was able to begin his calculations, from the completion of that first second of time, with that calculated speed that had balanced the earlier Macuzio equation.

The diameter of the concentrated 'ball' of electro-magnetic energy, released by the Big Bang, had at the end of that first second of time, already grown greater than 1.2 million miles. From that second on, the speed of light had slowly declined. The enormous tension created in space, as energy streaked into the void, began the process of conversion to matter, at an exceedingly rapid pace. As massive amounts of matter (hydrogen) formed, so gravity came into being, and as Einstein contended, 'gravitation slows down light'. (Confirmed by the observed effects that gravity has on light, both micro-lensing, which bends light across space, and the absence of light from Black Holes, where it is not just slowed down by gravity, but stopped from escaping altogether).

Having grabbed their attention, as it were, he showed that some phenomena, which had been propounded over the years, could well have taken place under these circumstances, without contravening Einstein's principle. He was able to show a decline in the average speed, from that moment, of one mile per hour, per second, which leads one to the current speed of light. This rate of decline was one mile per second for every 19,874 years—an undetectable rate of change, well within the margin of measurement error. His base being Webb's alpha observations which effectively spanned aeons of time.

In general accord with Friedmann's statement 'the universe expands forever, gradually decelerating, but never quite stopping,' Christopher showed mathematically that the speed of expansion declined comparatively slowly in the early stages of the universe's development as its mass of matter was low. The rate at which the speed of light diminished, accelerated over time as more and more matters was created, so increasing the gravitational power of the universe. Finally, it slowed once more as a state of near equilibrium had now been reached. Where the rate of increase in the creation of matter and its gravitational power is virtually equalled and offset by the attenuation of gravity by the ever-growing distance between galaxies. The speed of light has now therefore virtually stabilised at its present value.

His calculations led him to the conclusion that the universe is now only 8.23 billion years old, rather than the 16 billion years currently envisaged. Christopher calculated that its diameter was probably about 33 billion light years.

Having finalised and submitted his thesis, he sent a copy to Dr Macuzio, in recognition of triggering his enthusiasm, and congratulating him on his courage for his pioneering work in the field of VSL theory. He also thanked him for the time he'd spent explaining some very fundamental concepts in Washington, as well as his subsequent and very helpful emails.

His thesis was judged to be very well argued and the maths exemplary. They admired the dauntless impudence of his proposition, yet still remaining in accord with Einstein's general and special theories, as well as the work of Friedmann.

He had taken a very fresh look at the facts, so far as they were known, and emerged with a revolution in cosmological thinking. In so doing it cut through and eliminated many of the complexities in what had gone before. It was in essence a simplification, relying almost entirely on the few observable and proven facts.

It was pure science, it was new, it was beautiful to their minds, and as exhilarating as a Beethoven symphony. In short it was brilliant, elegant and Dr Allen (as he would now be known) quite blew their minds.

Chapter Twelve
Marriage

Christopher Allen and Emmanuelle Theurgy were married, with a Nuptial Mass, at midday on Saturday 21st June, two years to the day, from the day they first met. They had their reception at the Compleat Angler, alongside the Thames at Marlow.

Thea had stayed with her father at Chris's grandparents the previous night. She spent the whole morning getting ready as well as getting nervous. The old white Rolls Royce they'd booked picked them up on time and in spite of the journey from Oxfordshire, they arrived at St Joseph's just five minutes late; Helen was her bridesmaid.

Two of her friends, Jane Zimmermann from school and Marian Leonard from university, had flown over from the USA. Alan Walton, a school friend of Christopher who had gone to Liverpool University to study Insurance and Pension fund Administration, was Chris's best man. Charles Welbeck, a fellow and tutor at Cambridge, who'd recognised Christopher's talent, had befriended him in his first term and become his mentor, was his special guest. Relatives were few, but two of Helen's closest friends were invited, along with friends of Chris's parents, two of whom had taught him and Helen at their parent's schools.

Alan Walton's speech was very traditional as was Mr Theurgy's 'father of the bride speech', but in his case he'd spent hours over getting it just right. It was amusing when talking of Thea's early life, sad when he talked about the loss of her mother, but throughout its content, the great love that he had for his daughter shone through.

Chris's speech was not as polished as Manny's. He thanked everyone collectively for their wedding presents, which would be the start of their home in Cambridge. He thanked Manny for fathering such a stunning and wonderful bride, his parents, their friends, Charles Welbeck and his colleagues for educating him, and Helen for being there for him over the years. The surprise came at the end—their book *publisher* (name to be inserted) had given Manny six advance copies, due to be officially published on 1st July. Both he and Manny had signed four of them. He presented one to Thea, one to his mother, one to his father and one to Helen. He thanked each of them for their help in determining quite a lot of its content.

They all enjoyed a beautifully prepared meal; great wines and, after the speeches, retired to enjoy the sunshine on the lawn alongside the Thames, for coffee.

Later there was dancing, more wine and champagne, and to the surprise of the English guests, the traditional American garter 'ceremony' which Manny subsequently explained, to those who enquired, its history and meaning.

After all the guests had left, Chris and Thea retired, slightly nervously, to the hotel's honeymoon suite for the night. They need not have worried, they were at one with each other, consummating their marriage became a most wonderful experience.

Almost as soon as they were in the suite they embraced and kissed passionately, where before they had exercised great restraint, now they let themselves go where desire took them. They soon lay naked in bed; their hands caressing and exploring each other's body. Chris had marvelled at the beauty of Thea's body as she undressed for bed. Chris was the only man she had ever desired, her intensity of feeling growing from love, she'd proudly revealed herself to him. Her previous abstention was rewarded in her first carnal knowledge of him; his youthfully strong body and the hardness of his manhood were a revelation beyond her imagining.

They moved ahead in their lovemaking cautiously, each wanting to give rather than take pleasure. Finally, she mentally begged to give up her virginity, as, for the first time in her life, she experienced a man entering her body. Initially Chris moved gently within her, the pace quickening as their mutual desire moved towards its climax. The ultimate orgasm was truly awesome after all the waiting and anticipation, a dividend of true love that would now, hopefully, be oft repeated.

They slept in each other's arms, Thea's head resting on Chris's chest, both subconsciously aware of sharing their bed. Christopher woke quite early and took great pleasure just looking at Thea's beauty as she lay by his side. He could not resist gently caressing her body as memories of their first lovemaking suffused his mind. He marvelled at how lucky he was to have such a gorgeous wife.

When Thea finally woke at his gentle touch, her heart leapt at the sight of her husband so close to her, and at the memory of their lovemaking. She embraced him warmly saying, "Chris, last night was so wonderful, wake up my whole body by making passionate love to me again, I want you and need you so much." Christopher was not yet skilled at the art of lovemaking, but his love and desire to please Thea, guided his every move; it became the perfect start to the first full day of their married life together.

After their heart rates had finally slowed down in each other's sated embrace, they showered together, experiencing the pleasurable feel of washing each other's bodies for the first time. They laughingly helped to dry each other, put on their night clothes for the first time, opened the curtains to enjoy the river view and called room service to order breakfast.

They left the hotel about ten o'clock and drove to Chris's parents for a very light lunch, after opening and listing all their wedding presents. Eugene, Pat and Helen had taken the presents home with them the previous evening to keep until their return from honeymoon. Over lunch the conversation was sporadic, it was clear they were very happy, but wrapped up in each other, almost to the exclusion of the rest of the world. His parents did not want to break the spell, as it were, so they thoughtfully suggested that Helen should drive them to Heathrow for their 4:00 pm flight to Boston.

The BA flight was on time and it was just after 7:00 pm local time when they took a taxi to her previous home. Chris carried the cases into the house, and up to the bedroom. Christopher had bought first class and open return tickets for their honeymoon flights, so they'd already eaten very well.

They phoned their parents to report their safe arrival, unpacked, had great fun showering together again and were in bed by nine. The fact that it was 2:00 am English time was not the only reason.

The following morning, Monday, they went shopping locally to stock up a little with food and had brunch out. When they got home, they sat and wrote thank-you letters for all their presents, which they then posted. Duty done; their time was now entirely their own. They decided on an afternoon siesta, the mutual excuse being that it would help them to stay up till a normal hour that evening and thus help make the time change. They were blissfully happy and relaxed making love, followed by pillow talk of their future hopes and plans— finally they fell asleep. That evening they took Thea's car and went out to a bijou restaurant she knew for an intimate dinner.

On Tuesday afternoon they left Thea's car in the Logan Airport car park and flew down to Savannah. They took a taxi to the Mariner's Inn on Hilton Head Island where they stayed for six days. They played tennis, strolled on the beaches, swam in the Atlantic and sunbathed just a little, due to Thea's fair skin. They tried their hand at golf and visited some of the beautiful old houses for which Savannah was renowned. They walked in the willow-pattern style hotel gardens and occasionally sat at tables under sunshades for an aperitif before dinner. Most evenings, after dinner they returned to their spacious room with a balcony overlooking the sea and made gentle love.

On Monday 30th they hired a car and spent two leisurely days driving down the coast road through Jacksonville and Daytona Beach to Cape Canaveral, staying at motels. While there they were fortunate to experience the awesome power a

'Saturn' rocket launch. On Wednesday they drove to Orlando to visit Epcot, this time booking into a four-star hotel. On Thursday they took a flight from Orlando's Kissimmee airport to New Orleans. On Sunday they continued on to Los Angeles where they were booked to stay for four nights on the old Queen Mary, now berthed in the harbour as a hotel and restaurant.

The final part of their honeymoon travels consisted of another leisurely two-day drive on the beautiful coastal route 1 up to San Francisco. After another two days of sightseeing they flew back to Boston on Monday 14th July. They arrived back somewhat travel weary but excited and happy at all they had seen and done. Now they 'chilled out' for five days, catching up with the family by phone, beginning to live a more normal married life, before the only other commitment they had to fulfil. This was a one-day book signing in New York, at the publisher's expense, to help publicise its launch. Manny had agreed to do the same in London. The publishers planned for them to do the same thing in two weeks' time, but with each in their own country, for those who would like their book signed by both authors.

They flew down to New York where they were booked once again in the Manhattan Hilton. The publisher's agent collected them at 9:00, taking them to the bookshop. He introduced them to the manager and they got Chris settled at the signing table. The agent then took Thea shopping for a belated wedding present, saying he would meet Chris in the restaurant across the street for lunch at 12:30.

Dr Allen was very happy with the comments and compliments of the many customers; the three hours flew by. He got up for his hour's break a little after 12:30, as he went out to the street, he saw Thea and the agent just approaching the restaurant so took a quick look up the street and dashed across to meet them.

The truck driver didn't stand a chance. In one of those momentary lapses of concentration he'd looked the wrong way before dashing across. There was a squeal of brakes as the truck hit him, his momentum carried him into the path of a taxi coming in the opposite direction, its driver had already started to apply his brakes, but he also was too near to stop.

Thea screamed and ran into the road as the traffic came to a standstill. She sat on the road by him, taking his head gently into her arms. The agent dialled 911 on his mobile for an ambulance, the bookshop manager came running, alerted by the squeal of brakes. Thea could see Chris was in great pain when he opened his eyes. Blood was trickling from his mouth as he tried to speak, she heard nothing, but recognised the words "I love you" by lip reading alone. Thea sat with him in her arms, tears of sorrow streaming down her face. When the ambulance arrived, the paramedics gave him a shot of morphine before examining or attempting to move him.

The truck had hit his chest, breaking some ribs, which had pierced his left lung; the taxi had crushed his pelvis; he died in Thea's arms there, on the street, a few minutes later. Thea was heartbroken, a widow bereft.

Chapter Thirteen
Legacy

A great deal had happened in the two months since Christopher's death, in New York. Thea was once again living with her father in Boston, still lamenting the loss of Christopher, but her religious faith helped her in slowly coming to terms with his sudden death.

Paul Curtis had collected her from the bookshop manager's office and had taken her back to the Hilton. From there he'd phoned her father and her husband's parents, on her behalf, to tell them the terrible news; they'd been due to fly back the following day. At her request he also contacted her friend from university, Marian Leonard, asking her to meet Thea at Logan Airport. Thea was still in shock and somewhat aimless, so he packed Dr Allen's things while helping Thea to pack hers. He then took Mrs Allen to the airport, saw her through check-in and onto the plane for Boston.

Marian was devastated at the news, for she'd been at the wedding, and immediately agreed to meet Thea. When they met in Logan Airport, Marian cried as she held Thea in her arms, trying to comfort her and ease her sobs. When she got Thea home, she gave her a sedative and stayed the night.

Next morning, at Thea's request, she took her to church; she was by nature deeply religious and found some solace in her Sunday attendance at mass. When they returned home, Marian prepared a small breakfast, telling, Thea that she must eat something. Over the meal Marian got Thea to think about the decisions she must make regarding the immediate future. They gently discussed the alternatives between bouts of tears; Thea's wishes finally emerged.

She wanted Christopher's body flown to England to be buried in Maidenhead—she wanted him to be in his hometown. She would follow a day or two later; she needed time to gain better control of her emotions. She wanted to ask, via Marian, if she could stay with the Allen family until after the funeral. After that she would probably go to Cambridge to sort out the house question. Beyond that she didn't want to think, but would discuss anything else with them when she was there.

Marian phoned Thea's father and Chris's parents that afternoon, to discuss Thea's wishes. Her father had originally wanted to fly over to help his daughter, but had held off for 24 hours at Paul Curtis's suggestion. He decided he would now wait for her to come to England in the next two or three days. Christopher's parents had dearly hoped that Thea would make the decisions she had in fact made, and agreed to make all the arrangements for the funeral.

Marian stayed a second night and, in the morning, phoned her employer to say she would be absent for a day and why. She then phoned Paul Curtis to get the whereabouts of Christopher's body and proceeded to go through all the formalities needed to get his body flown to England. The two first class open returns Thea held, were more than enough to cover the cost. Marian also booked Thea onto the Thursday early morning flight to London. It took some time, but eventually, that afternoon, she was able to phone Chris's parents once more with all the details.

The Allen household was understandably subdued; there was little conversation, each preoccupied with their thoughts, comforting one another and slowly coming to terms with their grief. The requiem mass at St Joseph's was on Tuesday 29th July, followed by the internment at Braywick cemetery.

Charles Welbeck, his mentor at Cambridge who'd known him for the last few years, gave the eulogy. He began rather poignantly:

"I was privileged to be invited to Christopher and Thea's wedding just over five weeks ago, and am now privileged, but very, very sad indeed to be asked to say something about his unexpectedly short life."

He said he knew how much Christopher loved and admired Thea; he had felt they were kindred spirits from the moment they met at Stonehenge. He also knew that Christopher felt privileged that such a lovely lady had agreed to marry him.

He spoke of the time and effort invested by all parents in raising their children; their aspirations for their children's future, and the deep shock and sorrow that comes from the loss of a child. Short though his life was, they could be very proud of his achievements, many did not achieve what he'd managed to do, in their whole lifetime.

He talked of his brilliant academic career. From a sound education in his father's school, he obtained a double first at Cambridge, topped off, as it was, by his doctoral thesis. Charles had reproduced that thesis on the internet, and only now therefore was it beginning to be appreciated for its brilliance, by others. Charles had termed it 'The Creation Theory,' due to the opening statement of the thesis. This reflected a slight enigma; as a scientist Christopher was a surprisingly religious man, having chosen to become a Catholic just last Easter.

He quoted from the first review of his thesis that had appeared in the New Scientist. "Dr Allen has built a revised yet brilliant cosmological structure on the cornerstones of Einstein and Friedmann, it remains to be seen if it stands the scrutiny of his peers; the test of time. I'm inclined to think it will."

For a young man of twenty-five to have produced such sound and pioneering work in the abstruse field of what was termed VSL theory, to have obtained a doctorate and to have co-authored a book with his father-in-law, is a quite startling testament to what he would have gone on to achieve, if he had been spared.

During the days that followed Thea said goodbye to her father at Heathrow, he could no longer extend his leave of absence. Christopher's parents let Thea go through all his things, papers, clothes, books and other possessions.

His bank balance, which was now hers, came as a surprise. He still had over £165,000 left of his grandparent's legacy, and this was after paying £180,000 on the house. From their conversations before and during their lengthy honeymoon, she knew he was comfortably off, but the amount still came as a surprise.

The only other papers she wanted to keep related to his early work on the document and the love-letters she'd sent.

She also asked Pat if she would let her have a few photos of him in his earlier life and to let her take a few mementos.

Thea had made an appointment with Mr Johnson Jr. of Johnson, Johnson & Wilberforce, for Monday afternoon. They were the solicitors whom she and Chris had appointed to do the conveyancing on the house, while they were away on honeymoon.

Thea left Maidenhead in the morning to drive up to Cambridge in what had been Christopher's Golf GTI. She had a lighter moment. This car was called a 'Rabbit' in the USA; it was white—was that from Alice in Wonderland or Alice in the looking glass? Mr Johnson expressed his condolences when they met in his office; he noticed the pallid face and lack of exuberance in Mrs Allen, since their last meeting.

"Your husband left me a cheque to cover the £180,000 deposit on the house, our fees and a contingency. Surprisingly, for builders, they were almost on time, we actually completed the purchase on Friday 4th July—it was all straightforward. In your extended absence I took the liberty of making the first mortgage payment and insured the mortgage out of the money your husband left me.

"After I got your sad call last week, I checked with the insurance company. Once they receive a copy of the death certificate they will pay-off the mortgage under the terms of the insurance, the house will then be yours; I'll give you the keys when you leave."

She was absolutely stunned that the house was hers. She thanked him profusely, saying she had all her documents in a case in the trunk of her car; she'd leave the death certificate with him to obtain a copy.

"How much of Chris's cheque is left, or do I owe you some money?"

"A little over £470 is left, I think, we can finalise the account in the next couple of days and let you have a cheque for the balance. Have you decided what you're going to do with the house?"

"I don't know, so don't settle the account just yet. I'll probably go and look at it later this afternoon to help me decide. I'm going to stay in Cambridge for two or three days anyway, as I've got other things I need to attend to. I'll let you know before I leave."

Thea got a room in a local hotel, phoned her in-laws to let them know where she was and went to see her house. It was bare, but quite nicely finished, in line with what she and Chris had requested. The show house was still on the unfinished site, so to refresh her memory of what it might be like furnished, she went to look round it again.

That evening she phoned her father and then Charles Welbeck to let them know she was in Cambridge. Charles told her after the funeral that he'd collected together all Chris's papers, those he'd left in Cambridge and those he wanted to keep for his return, when taking up his job as a part-time tutor and member of Stephen Hawking's cosmological team. Charles took the opportunity to invite Thea to dinner with him and his wife, for the following evening, so she could collect the folders.

On Tuesday Thea had a look round the main shopping centre of the city as part of helping her to come to a decision about the future. She also returned to the estate agents through which they'd bought the house. The staff were very sorry to hear the news of Dr Allen's death and assumed Thea had come to put the house back on the market.

"I haven't decided what to do yet, could I perhaps let it, to give me an income?"

"Oh yes, that's very possible, quite a number of people are doing it, we have a few that we already manage. The rent generally pays the mortgage, but it would be pure income for you. It's also a good investment, property values invariably rise in the longer term. You'd have to furnish it of course."

They discussed the level of rent she could expect and then she left saying she would think about it and be in touch when she'd reached a decision.

Her next stop was a drugstore; it was very unusual for her to be overdue by a week. She'd started to feel a little strange, particularly in the morning; her heart had leapt with joy at the thought she might be pregnant with Christopher's child.

As she continued through the shopping area, back towards the car park, a book display in of a branch of Ottakar's caught her eye. Moving closer she knew why it had caught her attention, it was a pyramid of *Twenty-One Steps of Time* an introductory promotion. She entered the shop and enquired about the book. She didn't want to introduce herself, so asked if it would make a good present for her father?

"Well, it's starting to sell quite well. I've only just started reading it myself; it's quite interesting and rather unusual, I think he'd probably like it."

"I'll take one then, please" she said, thinking to give it to Charles that evening.

She drove to the house once more, warming to the idea of letting. If she was pregnant, the income would be very welcome and a growing house value would also be a good investment. Then, returning to her hotel she showered and changed then found her way to Charles' house with the aid of a map she'd purchased.

His wife was pleasant, commiserated with her loss, then offered her a drink, which helped her relax. She hardly registered eating the meal, because she found herself asking Charles lots of questions about Christopher, getting a clearer picture of his academic side for the first time. Charles's answers painted another side of Christopher; it also gave her more than a glimpse of life in Cambridge.

Over coffee, Charles asked her what life was like at Harvard, Chris had told him of her BA in business administration—how did it compare? It seemed, from the discussion that followed, that university life wasn't too different on the other side of the Atlantic. When she left, Charles helped her load Chris's papers into the back of the car. She thanked them both for a very pleasant and informative evening, handing Charles the copy of *Twenty-One Steps of Time* from the back of her car.

The next day she spent going through Chris's papers in her room. She quietly shed tears over some of them as they heightened her sense of loss. Many she did not understand, those relating to the development of his thesis. Needing a break, she phones room service for coffee, then having collected herself once more, she continued with the folders.

The most poignant time came as she read through two folders of papers relating to the document, vividly recalling their first meeting at Stonehenge. The first contained the original document and all his early notes, lots of other notes on random subjects followed, finally there were three sets of notes that were not his. One was from his grandfather on the subject of agriculture, one from his sister on medicine and one from his mother on religion; how odd she thought.

The second folder was much thinner than the first. He'd written eight essays, each relating to one aspect of the decrees listed in the second half of the document. She now saw the relevance of the 'random' notes and those other three sources. They were his research and the contributions from his grandfather, Pat and Helen; they were the groundwork for the essays. She was surprised he'd found the time to continue work on the document.

She needed another break to collect herself once more, this time she went for lunch in the hotel. As she was eating her waiter came to say there was a call for her, he'd take her meal and keep it hot for her. When she entered the booth in reception and picked up the phone, it was Pat.

"How are things Thea, have you seen the house? Gene and I are a bit worried about you being on your own. It's bad enough for us; we don't want you getting all depressed."

"Yes, I've seen the house, I like it, but I don't think I want to live there, it was for us, not me. I'm working through the pain of loss mum, I've had some tears, but I find strength from my faith. I had dinner with Charles and his wife yesterday evening and learnt a lot about Chris's academic life. He'd left a lot of his papers here, Charles gave them to me, and I've spent the morning going through them."

"Have you decided what you're going to do yet?"

"Not yet, but things are slowly beginning to clarify in my mind."

"The reason I called is because a man named Timothy Paine from the Daily Telegraph phoned us. He's doing a review of the book this weekend, he also wanted to speak to you. We didn't give him your number, but said we'd call you and you'd phone if you felt up to talking to him."

"That was very thoughtful of you mum, thanks. Did he chat to you; what did he want to know?"

"Yes we chatted; he was astonished and very sorry to hear that Chris had been killed. He was just after some background to the book really. We said you were better placed, knew more about it than us—he was your husband and the co-author is your father."

"Thanks again mum. By coincidence I saw a promotional display of them in a bookshop yesterday. Give me his number, I'll call him when I've finished my lunch."

"Oh! I'm sorry, I didn't know you were in the middle of it, sorry." She gave Thea Tim's number and said, "You get back to your lunch; please stay in touch."

"Of course, I will mum, bye for now."

"Tim Paine."

"Mr Paine, this is Mrs Allen; you wanted to speak to me?"

"Oh! Thanks for calling, I was so sorry to hear of your loss. I guess as you've called you are prepared to chat a little?"

"Yes of course, I was pleased to hear you were doing a review of their book and would like to help if I can."

"Great. I've only got a few questions, is that all right?"

"Sure, as long as you keep off painful topics."

"Of course. You are obviously American, I gather you lived over there with your father, what does he do when he's not writing?" …and so it went on for just a short while.

"Thanks Mrs Allen, you've been very helpful, I wish you all the best for the future."

On Thursday, Friday and Saturday, Thea began her shopping for carpets and furniture, light fittings, curtains and other furnishings. Then came kitchen appliances, cooker, fridge, washing machine and dish washer, pots, pans and other kitchen utensils, and so on. She focused on ex-stock products for delivery to the house from Monday onwards.

On Saturday she also picked up a copy of the Daily Telegraph and when she got back to her hotel, scanned the Arts + Books supplement until she found the *Twenty-One Steps of Time* review.

'In some ways it's a complex book, but eminently readable in style. Based on an outline by Christopher Allen it speaks on many different levels. The ethereal and spiritual, the speculative and theoretical, biblical and philosophical, the evolutionary and the creative.

'Its primary thrust is making a case to reconcile evolution with the act of creation as told in the bible. The key to this being the introduction of two distinct forms of being, Humankind and Mankind, the latter created by humankind being imbued with a soul.

'Christopher Allen unfortunately was killed in a tragic road accident in New York in July, aged twenty-five. He had just obtained a doctorate at Cambridge when he married last June, one year after gaining a double first in math and physics.

'The first chapter of the book reflects a laicised version of his 'Creation Theory' which, I understand, is starting to receive critical acclaim from some of his peers. Apparently it changes how we should view the universe, reducing its existence to almost half of what was previously thought, yet making its size somewhat greater. I'm reliably informed that it's a reasoned revision to accepted cosmological thinking, as laid down by Einstein and Friedmann.

'In the prologue he makes a statement, as if it is a quote from God. He elaborates on this to say why God not only made the universe, but also why he made it the way it is—life and death, good and evil, triumph and disaster, an eternal cycle of change. He introduces us to the nineteenth century philosophical work of Charles Kingsley in the process Dr Allen also introduces the idea of ever-shortening steps of time for the life of this world. But it begs the question, why and to what end. It was not an intended pun, but if one were to progress this unusual concept of time, then the world would end in the year 3914 AD! Neither Dr Allen nor Mr Theurgy offers any valid explanation for this approach, other than a somewhat abstruse comment in the Foreword.

'The rest of the book is unusual for a totally different reason, it was written by his father-in-law—Emmanuel Theurgy. He lives in Boston and is a senior member of staff at the Peabody Museum of Archaeology, part of Harvard University. He incorporates all the latest and sometimes fascinating ideas, theories and facts about what is known of the Earth's evolution.

'Some readers may recall another unusual book that made the best seller list some years ago, *A Brief History of Time* by Stephen Hawking. This new book might well join it by giving us an insight into our existence. I recommend it to anyone with an interest in astronomy, evolution or religion.'

On Sunday, after church, Thea spent some time on the phone to her father in Boston and her in-laws in Maidenhead. She explained that she had decided to furnish and let the house; she anticipated it might take about two weeks. She would then like to come to Maidenhead for a couple of days before rejoining her father in Boston.

On the Monday she rose early, checked out of the hotel and went to the house to let in the carpet fitters; from there on it was all go. She arranged for a phone to be put in, saw the site foreman to organise the electrical fitting work, the putting up of curtain rails and plumbing-in the kitchen appliances. Little did she realise that her American accent, good looks and pleasant manner, along with what appeared to be her single status, played a key part in this. She spent time receiving and placing all she had bought, directing the workmen on what to fix or fit and where, as well as making cups of tea and coffee. She also did a little local grocery shopping as she had now moved in.

By the middle of the second week the inside of the house began to look the way she had originally intended in her mind's eye. As fitting out this home neared completion she made three further visits in Cambridge. She went to see Mr Reed at the estate agents to place it letting in his hands. She then went to Mr Johnson the solicitor to ask him to draw up any letting contract, saying she would be returning to Boston, then gave him a cheque for £530 to make a £1,000 deposit for his services. Finally, she put £100,000 on deposit with Building Society; it was the best interest rate she found and significantly better than the rates in the USA.

During the last week, unbeknown to Thea, the book publishers had noted the climbing sales of *Twenty-One Steps of Time*. In the tradition of all good marketing they had decided to generate further publicity, get behind the growing sales trend, and push. An obvious element in public relations is the author, so they contacted Emmanuel Theurgy in Boston.

By Friday the house was ready to let, so she booked her flight to Boston for the following Monday afternoon. Later in the day she drove to Maidenhead to revisit Eugene, Pat and Helen, after dropping the keys off at the estate agents.

She was greeted warmly and made to feel at home. When she brought in her overnight case she asked Pat if she could use Christopher's bedroom; Pat was rather surprised, but readily agreed. Helen was also at home, on holiday from Imperial College, it being the end of her first year. They were not yet over the shock of losing Christopher, but were now able to talk about him a little, without bursting into tears.

Then Thea asked to be excused for retiring a little early, as she was still a bit tired from the hard work of the last two weeks. Thea had guessed that Pat would not have cleared Christopher's room yet.

Surrounded with his possessions, as she had wanted, Thea tossed and turned as she thought a lot about him and what he would want her to do. She had a few tears, but finally her mind cleared when she recalled going through the papers Charles Welbeck gave her. The eight essays came to the forefront of her mind. She didn't know how or when he'd found the time to do all the research and then to write them as well?

They put flesh on the bones of the decrees listed in the second half of the document. Three were based on the notes from his grandfather, Pat and Helen.

When she got up, she went out with Pat and Helen for a light lunch and a walk round the shops in Windsor. It gave her the opportunity to buy each of them, including Eugene, a nice present for putting her up and one to take back for her father.

That evening over dinner she told them about the baby, Christopher Junior and spoke more about Christopher, the Christopher she had known and loved.

"I'm so grateful to have experienced our married life, short though it was. Our love was deep-rooted; our honeymoon was superb, it far exceeded all my expectations. I will treasure those four weeks and five hours for the rest of my life. Obviously, I didn't expect it to end so soon, or quite so suddenly.

"Christopher was standing very near me in the crowd at Stonehenge, I noticed him because he seemed to go into a momentary trance, and his head was surrounded in what I can only describe as St Elmo's fire. In that same moment a paper appeared and wrapped itself on his leg, caught in a gust of wind. Also, at that very same moment the first rays of the sunrise appeared, then the moment had passed, Chris moved and saw me. It was then that I really knew he was my man.

"He told me something similar on our honeymoon, he knew in the same moment he saw me, that I was to be his wife. When he asked me, what had brought me to Stonehenge, I surprised myself with an unbidden thought, I said 'I came to meet you', we ended up having breakfast together.

"What Christopher told me, and me alone, very much later in our courtship, because he would have been too embarrassed, was that he'd had a vision. In that trance-like moment of stillness he'd seen God; he'd seen Satan banished from heaven and he'd heard God say the words he used in the beginning of the book's preface. Where He explains why He made the universe, and us; he said time stood still; it was a truly awesome experience.

"He was far too modest to think it anything other than a daydream, until he came to believe in the veracity of the document. Even then he would not mention it, in the belief that others would think him boastful or even going mad, he remained amazed that he'd really had a vision.

"As it turned out, all of us helped him to decipher the document. As no doubt you noticed, mum, the work of Charles Kingsley proved to be key to his understanding. It was his work on the document that led him to develop his 'Creation Theory' and obtain his doctorate."

There was a stunned silence for a while as the implications of all that Thea had said began to sink in. They were comforted by what she'd told them, but, by the same token, found it very hard to come to terms with it all. Pat recognised the truth, Thea and Chris were special, Christopher knew that there was something unique about Thea, it was all meant to be.

On Sunday after mass, Thea and Helen went for a walk, they were not too far apart in age and their love of Christopher made a bond. Thea was pleased to hear how well Helen's medical studies had gone in her first year. Helen also talked of her love for 'Tong' who would qualify in a year's time. She hoped to persuade him to come to England for a holiday next year to meet her parents, a trip she would fund. If all went well, Helen wanted to marry Tong when she qualified and her ambition was to enter a medical practice with Tong, in Pattaya. She asked Thea not to tell mum and dad, quite a lot of water has to flow under the bridge first.

As a result of Helen talking about her work in the orphanage, Thea decided, as she was now quite well off, to do the same as Chris's parents and sponsor a child there. Soon after their return the phone rang, it was for Thea.

"This is Amelia Curtis from the London office of (must note *the name of book publishers to be inserted)*. I'm very sorry to trouble you on a Sunday but we wanted to be sure we caught you before you returned to Boston."

"How did you find me?"

"My American colleagues contacted your father to find out where you were. He said he thought you wouldn't mind, but he didn't know exactly when you planned to return."

"Oh! So why do you want to speak to me?"

"Your husband's and father's book is now off the shelves, we want to give it a further push, we'd like you to help if you would?"

"What will that entail?"

"We'd already organised to pre-record spots for Monday and Tuesday on Patrick Moore's 'Sky at Night', 'The Book Programme' on BBC digital, Channel 4 and an early morning slot on the BBC 'Today' programme on Radio 4. There might be others; your father is doing something similar in the States. You, as his daughter and the wife of Dr Allen, you would make an unusual but very interesting interviewee, far better than one of us doing it.

"Hold on a minute, would you." Covering the phone, she explained to Pat and asked if she could stay on until Thursday? Pat said of course she could. Going back to the phone Thea said, "I can do what you ask up to Wednesday afternoon if you organise transport, but I must go back to Boston on Thursday."

"Oh! That's great, thanks. Yes I'll organise transport; we'll pick you up at 9:00 tomorrow morning. We can brief you more fully in the car and thanks again."

"You're welcome," and Thea put down the phone.

Turning to Pat and Helen she explained more fully, thanked Pat for letting her stay on and said she would phone BA to change her flight.

Thea quite enjoyed doing the rounds of various studios, once she'd got used to it, in fact she was kept quite busy for most of the three days meeting an interesting range of people. Christopher would have been far better she thought, but her good looks, particularly on TV, did a great deal for the book's promotion.

She discovered that Christopher's name was becoming quite well known. Through the book, his Creation Theory, what he had achieved at such a young age and the ghoulish fact that he was killed on the very last day of their honeymoon. It was not all plain sailing however, on the 'Sky at Night' she discovered that his Creation Theory was not universally accepted, some cosmologists found it too simplistic, she thought they enjoyed the complexities that had been woven over the years, in their view they could not be so easily dismissed.

Once she was on the plane to Boston, she looked back on all the recent events in her life. She managed to adopt a positive attitude, no longer feeling so sorry for herself, but starting to count her blessings. There would be the income from Chris's share of the royalties on the book, the house rent from Cambridge, the interest from the 'Building Society' bond and the £50,000 that remained. By living rent-free with her father meant she could easily raise her baby without needing to take a job until he was at school, and then probably would only need to get a part-time job. She would, at the same time, be able to keep house, and look after her father properly.

The reunion with her father at Logan Airport was a very tearful affair; they had not seen each other since the funeral. He had been concerned as to how much she was still hurting, but when she whispered in his ear that she was expecting Chris's baby, a lot of the clouds began to clear.

In the main they settled back into their previous way of life. Thea spent her time decorating, preparing a nursery, and slowly gathering together all that modern mothers seem to need for the next generation.

Chapter Fourteen
Conversation

Manny, Thea, Pat and Eugene spoke at least once a week on the phone. They comforted one another, slowly recovering from the loss of Christopher. Initially they would talk of memorable moments in Christopher's life; Thea's preparations for the coming of Chris Jnr; how Helen was doing at Imperial College etc. A time passed they all began to speak of the fact that the task given them, was, by no means complete.

Thea said we have all spent many hours discussing with each other all that flowed from her meeting with Christopher at Stonehenge. We have all come to recognise that the task given to us has not ended with Christopher's "Creation Theory" and his doctorate. The four of us must decide how best to try to implement the second half of the Document.

Pat thought they alone had no chance. They must do their best, but God may well have taken many other steps, across the world, to prompt needed change. She felt their role, to reverse the steepening decline of mankind's moral standards was way beyond their abilities; what they should do is convince the church to take the initiative. To do this we must first clarify our thinking, to make a convincing presentation;

I think we should email each other of what we might say so we can martial our joint thinking; they agreed.

Thea sent the first email: I think we take Christopher's vision very seriously. I can at least do what he told me on our honeymoon. My interpretation is that God showing Chris what happened to Satan and his followers is now happening to his followers here on Earth—"soul yield falling." We can all at least to the fact that we now believe the Document is genuine; a direction to us on what must be undertaken.

The church takes visions very seriously, I have the original Document to give them, but we must have much more.

Pat wrote an email: Gene and I agree with Thea; we must try to understand God's intentions in sending us this Document. We talked round the subject for some time. Suddenly we went back a step—"Satan licensed"—the documents key word 'licensed.' A licence is given or sold but it can be revoked. This train of thought eventually led me to recall a passage in the Book of Revelation, it reads: *"I saw an angel come down from heaven, holding in his hand the key of the abyss, and a heavy chain. He seized the dragon, that ancient serpent—that is the Devil, or Satan—and chained him into the abyss, locked it, and sealed it, so that he could not deceive the nations anymore, until a thousand years were over."*

We discussed it and reached some outline conclusion. It struck us that it did not say God decreed, but he sent an angel, was this therefore at mankind's request? We also know, from Christopher's work, the world will last until the 40th millennium—well over a thousand years hence, plenty of time for this to happen.

Another train of thought in our discussion was the way in which God indicated that this is the final age. Jesus talks about the fig tree with green shoots that say summer is coming. About the red sky in the morning and in the evening indicating bad or good weather to come; or a North or South wind bringing cold or warm weather, but we cannot read the signs of the final age. Did Jesus say this to highlight that His coming was the beginning of the final age?

Jesus draws our attention to reading the signs that are now with us—the finite supplies of the world. He is forcing us to take action. I agree with Thea, we must enrol the church. Ours is a trans-Atlantic partnership; I suggest we plan to speak to our two diocesan bishops, and through them to activate the whole church. They, with Cardinals and the Pope must ask God, in prayer, to lock-up Satan. They must also ask what momentous action they must take to initiate change in mankind's behaviour.

Manny wrote an email: I have spent many hours wondering how it is that mankind has suddenly, and so rapidly, steeped its descent towards Satan's abyss. I have concluded that two interlinked events have been the cause: The internet and women prioritising employment in place of child rearing—each has occurred over the last 80 years since World War II.

Every kind of sexual depravity has become freely available, any time, any place. It corrupts minds, is available to children, now such things are seen as the norm! It is also the driving force that causes adults to become debased. It does Satan's work; child abuse has spread rapidly, now it is emerging that even clergy have succumbed to the siren call.

This insidious decline in morals has been enhanced by an even more insidious change: women going out to work; children being raised in nurseries, not by parental love, older children coming home from school to an empty house, free to go on the internet and do as they please—they are growing up without parental loving care. We are now seeing the third generation bringing the children into the world not knowing how to raise them properly with little love; no wonder they are going "off the rails." The raising of children, in a loving environment, to at least the age of seven, should be the norm; giving them the do's and the don'ts of life.

Paul Johnson, writing in the 'Spectator' put the situation far better than I ever could. The modern world Freud, Hitler and Stalin, it is Auschwitz and the Gulag, it is Aids and anorexia, crack and speed, Hiroshima and the killing fields, San Francisco butt houses and Bangkok brothels. At its miserable best it is down market tabloids, Disneyland and channel for porn. As its worst it is human degradation so complete, and cruelty so heartless as to leave Satan and his pandemonium gasping with pride at their creation. For it is they who brought the modern world into this depraved existence.

Instead of a loving environment, two key aspects of life have been handed to school teachers: religion and sex. The former, is covering the range of major religions, sows confusion; the latter sows the desire to experiment—both yet another road to disaster.

"The genie is out of the bottle; it is only God that can put it back. I applaud Pat's suggestion that we pray that God will lock-up Satan. All we can hope to do is what John Wilkins wrote in *The Tablet*: 'One must warn the gullible multitude about the abyss of grief to which the modern world inevitably leads'."

Pat and Gene sent an email: Manny, I can see how each generation is less well equipped to pass on moral leadership. Each generation has been left to grow up with no sense of direction, no real purpose. I whole heartedly agree with you.

I feel now, we must turn our attention to the second half of the Document—The Remedial Actions Decreed. It is clearly up to us to take the initiative; I have two suggestions.

The first is that Christopher wrote eight essays, covering the subject matter, all conjecture about future life on earth, how it would unfold, based on the foundation stones of the past. I feel Manny, after your joint book "The Steps of Time", a second book, would be a very worthwhile endeavour. If you could expand on Christopher's essays, as you so ably did on the world's evolution, but add in how you see the major change we seek, coming about, it would go a long way towards influencing change. Another joint authorship that brings readers hope. A big ask for you to think about.

The second suggestion is that we take the Document, and the actions that it has inspired, to the church hierarchy. As we live either side of the Atlantic we have two people we can approach; the bishops of the Boston and Portsmouth diocese. To give us time to prepare, I suggest that Gene and I come over to Boston at the end of March next year (we can see Christopher Jnr, our first grandchild, when he's born) to make a joint presentation to your Cardinal, Patrick O'Malley. Then you both bring Christopher Jnr to England about the 15th of June to make the same presentation to Bishop Crispian Hollis. This timing would enable us to organise Christopher Junior's baptism on the 21st, the anniversary of our wedding in St Joseph's.

As you gather, I think we must hand over all the evidence to the church, for then to carry the Document's message forward. The church is struggling to cope with the decline in numbers, the two main insidious reasons that Manny highlighted, that has had such a devastating effect on mankind. I feel only they, and God, can produce a worldwide solution.

The next email came from Manny and Thea. Your idea Pat, of two presentations to the church, via our bishops, gives us twice the opportunity to convince the church, through them, to think, evaluate and conclude the validity of our story, and determine a course of action. Your timing is brilliant. We have ample time to develop a succinct and meaningful presentation and visiting each other in the process, with its personal opportunities is a stroke of genius. We would love to have you here for Junior's arrival, and the idea of his baptism on Thea's wedding anniversary, beautiful. We can book a meeting with Patrick O'Malley and trust to God that is not the day Junior arrives. The meeting over there is automatically dictated by the baptism date.

Your other idea about a second book, I need to think about. Thea has all eight of Christopher's essays, which I have reread. Unlike the first book, putting flesh on the bones of the essays requires quite a big ask of conjectural imagination, but how I might meld the eight into the outcome of our work would be a huge leap in imagination. Don't get me wrong, I am not saying no, but I must give it lots of thought.

Turning to the presentations to our bishops, I think all four of us must have a role. I can introduce us, talk of Thea and

Christopher's meeting at Stonehenge, the book he and I published, and his death in New York.

Thea can attest to the events at Stonehenge, particularly his vision, and hand over the original Document. Pat can talk of Christopher's work in numbers and his development of his Creation Theory for which he obtained his doctorate. Gene can end with our developed view of the second half of the Document, and our conclusions, our request for prayer for the locking-up of Satan.

The dates were fixed with the bishops, then for the next few months they wrote, and rewrote many times, distilling it down to the essential points, then they were ready.

Chapter Fifteen
Handover

Manny started: Your Grace, this is Emmanuelle, my daughter, and these are her mother and father-in-law, Eugene and Patricia Allen. Christopher, their son, you may recall, was killed in New York on the last day of my daughter's honeymoon.

You may, perhaps, be aware of the book "The Steps of Time", published last year; written by Christopher and me.

The four of us are here because we have a God given series of events to hand over to the church.

Thea took over: Christopher and I, met at Stonehenge on the 21st June 2000. It was very unusual, when I first saw him he was momentarily in a trance—like state with an aura around his head. I am here to attest to the fact that he had a vision. He saw God expel Satan from heaven along with his pandemonium. What is more, a gust of wind wrapped this document (she handed it over) around his lower leg. It is written in Aramaic—here is a translation.

Christopher spent the rest of his summer holiday deciphering the meaning of the first part; dad, Pat, Gene and I assisted him in this task. Here is a folder containing his notes that led to his conclusions, and a doctorate at Cambridge University in England, last year.

Pat took over. Christopher's work dealt with the numbers in the first two parts of the document; we are here because we feel we must hand over the second half of the document to the church; you may well ask why?

Because we all have come to believe, from all that has happened since, that this is a genuine act of God, to bring about needed remedial action, and that we think it is the church's job.

Everyone now recognises that mankind is descending into an abyss of sinfulness. It is even now emerging that the church's priests and bishops are being tainted by child abuse allegations. Good priests in both our diocese are getting more and more depressed that not only are they "fighting" against decadence, but are, in some cases being attacked for their trouble. On top of which the church hierarchy is now also involved.

Gene took over. Addressing the second half of the document—Current Status and Remedial Action Decreed,—Christopher had started to consider this: He wrote eight essays; Manny, Mr Theurgy, has agreed to write a second book, putting flesh on the bones of Christopher's essays, as well as adding his view of the future.

We are here to ask the church, through you, to take action, to begin with prayers, asking God to implement the locking and chaining up Satan in the abyss, as given in the Book of Revelation. We believe it is up to mankind to ask this, recognising the need and praying that an angel is sent to do it.

Do you have any questions?

Patrick O'Malley addressed them: it is obvious, Mrs Allen that you are expecting a child, when is the baby due? Any day now, she replied, we are all convinced it will be a boy, I intend naming him Christopher, Eugene Emmanuel, after his father and both grandfathers. We plan to have him baptized in England, on the 21st of June, the first anniversary of my wedding.

That sounds wonderful Mrs Allen, thank you.

My next question to Mr and Mrs Allen is also personal. I know the background of Mr Theurgy and Mrs Allen, nee Theurgy, I had my secretary look into it before arranging this meeting. May I ask you to tell me something of you and your wife?

We are both teachers, my wife teaches religious education, I teach math. We were raised as Anglicans; we also have a daughter, Helen, who is studying medicine. As a result of all that has happened in the last five years we converted to Catholicism, a year ago last Easter, Helen became a convert in Thailand where she was working in an orphanage.

Thank you and congratulations; I have a third question. What are you expecting from this meeting?

Well, we hope and pray that you will believe what we now believe, and take the matter to the American Bishops Conference. We have already booked the 20th June to make the same presentation to Bishop Crispian Hollis in Portsmouth, as our endeavours have been a trans-Atlantic affair. On the 21st will be Christopher Junior's baptism at St Joseph's where Thea and our son were married.

We trust that Crispian Hollis will also take the matter to the English and Welsh Bishops Conference. If both conferences agree that our experience is reality, we pray that both of you will take it to the Pope.

xxxx

I am impressed with your sincerity. I will get the document scientifically examined; subject to that outcome, I then agree to do my part in taking it to our conference and to the Pope.

xxxx

Christopher Jnr. Was born the very next day, so all three grandparents were able to bond with the young boy.

Mr and Mrs Allen left for England and were followed two months later by Manny, Thea and Chris, overnight, on the 17/18th June.

On the 20th June, Gene drove them to St Edmond's House, Portsmouth to make the same presentation to Bishop Crispian Hollis. His reaction was similar to Patrick O'Malley's. He agreed to take it to the next bishop's conference of England and Wales in November. This was chaired by Archbishop Murphy O'Connor from the Westminster Diocese.

Christopher Eugene Emmanuel was baptized during the daily mass, by Fr Tom, at St Joseph's, Maidenhead the following day; the 21st June 2006.

Epilogue

The book you have just read was written in the period 2,000-2,004. When I reached this point I could not think of a satisfactory ending: finally I put the manuscript aside.

In 2019 a very, very satisfactory ending leapt out at me. Pope Francis sent out a request to all Catholic Clergy.

In my own words *"I want the prayer of St Michael said after every mass, every day, in every church throughout the world; prayed by the congregation led by the priest."*

This prayer reads as follows:

"Saint Michael the Archangel defend us in battle. Defend us against the wickedness of the devil and all his companions that roam around the world seeking the ruin of souls."

THE END

P.S. 15 years later; God doesn't work to our time.

Epilogue

I (Paul) know a certain Christian man who, fourteen years ago (Damascene moment) was snatched up to the highest heaven. I do not know whether this actually happened or whether he had a vision—only God knows.

(2 Corinthians 12:2)

Chapter Sixteen
Appendix I

The Document

Location:

- *Galaxy*—Sp 615,761,893—MW
- *Star*—CC27K
- *Planet*—03—4.110 /1—6/15—M21C

Current Status:

- *Satan licensed—Soul yield falling.*

Twenty-Third Phase (Start 1960-Finish 980)
Remedial Actions Decreed:

- *Increase agricultural output to ten billion level.*
- *Raise vulnerability awareness.*
- *Environment—material s—energy.*

After a suitable period:

- *Initiate new energy source.*
- *Apply medical knowledge limitation.*

- Provide additional communications capability.

- Permit inter-planetary travel only.

- When fully prepared—make final call to conversion.

Chapter Seventeen
Appendix II

The Book's Time Reference Table

The Thirty-Three Steps of Time			Earth's Calendar
		Years	*Years*
		16,441,671,680	
	(1)	8,220,835,840	
1	(2)	4,110,417,920	
2	(3)	2,055,208,960	
3	(4)	1,027,604,480	
4	(5)	513,802,240	
5	(6)	256,901,120	
6	(7)	128,450,560	
7	(8)	64,225,280	
8	(9)	32,112,640	
9	(10)	16,056,320	
10	(11)	8,028,160	
11	(12)	4,014,080	4,010,166
12	(13)	2,007,040	2,003,126
13	(14)	1,003,520	999,606
14	(15)	501,760	497,847
15	(16)	250,880	246,966
16	(17)	125,440	121,526

17	(18)	62,720		58,806
18	(19)	31,360		27,446
19	(20)	15,680		11,766
20	(21)	7,840	(Creation of Adam & Eve)	3,926
21	(22)	3,920	(Birth of Christ)	6 BC
22	(23)	**1,960**	**Start date— datum point**	1,954 AD
23	(24)	**980**	**Finish date— datum point**	2,934
24	(25)	490		3,424
25	(26)	245		3,669
26	(27)	122		3,791
27	(28)	61		3,852
28	(29)	31		3,883
29	(30)	15		3,898
30	(31)	8		3,906
31	(32)	4		3,910
32	(33)	2		3,912
33	(34)	1		3,913

Note: (xx) = The initial numbering of the steps of time.

Chapter Eighteen
Appendix III

Christopher's Notes on Creation

Do you know?
Were you not told long ago?
Have you not heard how the world began?

When God banished Satan from heaven, he said, "I will replace the fallen angels with new loyal beings who will not rebel—they will have earned their place with me. Those that do not will forever join the rebels, without ever setting foot in my kingdom."

At that moment, in His omniscience, He decided to create an evolving universe. A creation in which galaxies, stars, planets and creatures would evolve. By this means He chose to present mankind with the opportunity to earn a place with him in heaven, but at a cost. Death would be an inevitable part of this evolving universe, be they galaxies, stars, planets or people—each generation would have to give away to the next.

Mutations would be a necessary part, to generate new forms of existence; such mutations would be a necessary part, to generate new forms of existence; such mutations would range from good to bad. This kind of creation would allow for terrible events, not because God is callous, but because such a creation would necessarily be a place of change, ragged edges, blind alleys, transience and death.

It would cause mankind to reflect, to recognise God's power, to set a challenge and provide the opportunity to help one another. His ultimate purpose would be to provide a free choice for mankind to enter into a life with Him.

In the beginning, when God began to create the universe, eight billion, two hundred and twenty million, eight hundred and thirty-five thousand, eight hundred and forty years ago, God created a singularity. Where there was nothing, a singularity existed in that very first millisecond of time. The greatest event ever, the first instant of the first aeon, that began the creation of time, space and the universe. It was an unimaginably dense kernel of energy that seemingly burst from nowhere into the void, spreading out at phenomenal speed. The Earth did not exist; the explosion that was creating space was, as yet, formless and desolate.

Possibly two, three or perhaps even four times faster than the present speed of all radiant energy, God only knows. It streaked across the void like a hurricane. The space being created was like the raging ocean magnified many millions of times, a gigantic tempestuous fury. A maelstrom of energy that was engulfed in total darkness and it was like an awesome wind that was moving over the water, creating wave after wave of expanding space.

This stupendous burst of radiant energy was beyond comprehension, beyond any human imaging, beyond the concept of a billion tempestuous hurricanes. The speed of its spread across the void slowly diminished over time, due to gravity as the simplest of matter began to form—hydrogen, the least complex of the atoms, the first on the atomic scale, and the building block of the universe.

It took hundreds of thousands, maybe hundreds of millions, or perhaps even as much as a billion years, for countless trillions upon trillions of hydrogen molecules to fill the ever-expanding space. The great waves of energy created ripples, which caused the hydrogen to form into millions of clouds, some huge, some enormous, some immense! Then God commanded "Let there be light" and gravity had played its part. That was the moment that the speed of expansion stabilised at the current speed of light.

Gravity caused the clouds of hydrogen to begin to contract—extremely slowly at first. After perhaps a further two or three hundred million years, the more concentrated mass that was each cloud, produced an increase in the power of the gravitational force at its centre. Thus the process of galaxy formation began. The ever-increasing gravitational force generated increasing pressure within each cloud; in turn this caused the temperature to rise. Ultimately the temperature and pressure within each cloud became great enough for spontaneous nuclear reaction to begin, creating light—and light appeared.

The continuing nuclear reaction brought about the transmutation of hydrogen into helium; each cloud was like an awesome hydrogen bomb, making the second step along the elemental scale. As the magnitude of the nuclear reaction increased, feeding upon itself, it escalated until it made a second transition, transmuting helium into lithium, then came lithium into beryllium, beryllium to boron, boron to carbon, and so, on it went. It was the start of the building process that created the ninety-two natural elements of the periodic table. God was pleased with what he saw.

Then He separated the light from the darkness by creating rotation. Just as skaters increase their speed of rotation by drawing in their arms, so the clouds of gas began to slowly rotate as gravity increased their density reducing their overall diameter. Now referred to as the Coriolis force, it is a hypothetical force, postulated to explain this phenomena. This rotation is the universal mechanism that produces periods of light and dark, and *He named the light "Day" and the darkness "Night"*.

The cores of the denser clouds continued to build in intensity, eventually becoming boiling cauldrons of atomic energy in space, the nuclear reactions generating progressively heavier elements such as iron, cobalt, nickel, copper and zinc. These cores were being continuously fed by gravity, with ever more hydrogen from the immensity of the cloud surrounding each. This process continued inexorably as the increasing power of gravity attracted ever greater quantities of hydrogen.

Finally, the clouds became so dense that they formed "Black Holes", clouds so dense, where gravity had become so great, not even light could escape! The nuclear process produced even heavier elements such as molybdenum, tin, silver, caesium, barium, samarium and gold. The timescale of each cloud's development varied as a function of the original cloud size—all were pregnant galaxies in the making, at some future point in time, each with a differing gestation period.

As the Black Holes grew ever larger, they turned into Quasars, white-hot cauldrons of energy where the temperature rose immeasurably to millions of degrees. The elemental process continued, finally creating the elements at the heaviest end of the periodic table, such elements as mercury, lead, radium, thorium, and uranium. Bohrium (107), Hassium (108), Meitnerium (109) up to 118 with 113, 115 and 117 missing—last 9 no official names yet. 116 Livermorium, 117 Tennessine, 118 Oganesson.

This phenomenal maelstrom of boiling matter was, once again, beyond human imaging; it progressed to producing cocktails of elements, hundreds, and even thousands of combinations of chemicals and exotic compounds. With a virtually limitless supply of hydrogen in space, the building process continued relentlessly.

Eventually, the density became so great that the Black Holes progressed to form "Supermassive Black Holes," unimaginably large, dense and immense volumes of apparent darkness, but nonetheless a boiling, seething mass of elements, deep within.

When this unprecedented nuclear activity reached enormous proportions, when it became a maelstrom of violence reaching perhaps 20 million degrees centigrade, galaxy gestation was complete. The moment of birth had arrived; the Black Holes finally exploded into galaxies, first one, then another, until they grew to millions. Each was a truly massive explosion of enormous proportions that threw out great showers of suns, typically one to two hundred billion in a single galaxy! Our 'Milky Way' is one of these galaxies, alone measuring about one hundred thousand years in diameter!

The violence of this huge, enormously large explosion threw matter so far out that the residual Black Hole at its core could no longer "feed" on the matter surrounding it. The centripetal force of gravity was reduced by distance and was now balanced by the centrifugal force of rotation. Matter was now too far removed from the centre, and rotating too fast to be drawn back into the Black Hole at its centre.

From a gestation process lasting over three billion years, our sun was created within the 'Milky Way' some five billion years ago. It was thrown out about 27,000 light years from the centre of our galaxy; onto what is the inner edge of one of the arms of our spiral galaxy called 'Carina Centauri.' The nearest sun to ours is the star 'Proxima Centauri', about four and a half light years away.

In addition to all the stars, there was a host of smaller matter, white-hot fragments, thrown out in the explosion. Unlike the suns, these were not large enough to maintain nuclear fission. Some of this matter circled our sun, and became the building material of Earth and the other planets. The larger pieces were massive enough to attract smaller pieces by gravity, so building the eight planets of our solar system, from Mercury to Neptune. Our Earth formed in this way some four point six billion years ago. It was the beginning of what we now called the Archeozoic Period of the Precambrian Era.

All the planets were white-hot balls of bubbling matter in space, they slowly cooled, the rate dependant on how far they were from the sun, and on how much radioactive material they contained. The faster cooling outer layer of our Earth, exposed to the frigidity of space, slowly formed a crust. The crust finally became deep enough and strong enough to withstand the impact of smaller rocks which were attracted to it. This prevented such meteorites from shooting into the molten core of the Earth. The oldest of these found has been carbon-dated at 4.55 billion years old. The Earth's crust finally became cool enough, deep enough, rigid enough and strong enough for God's plan—the beginning of the next step in His evolving creation.

In total, four billion, one hundred and ten million, four hundred and seventeen thousand, nine hundred and twenty years had passed—half of all time.

Evening passed and morning came—that was the first day.

Then God commanded "Let there be a dome to divide the water and to keep it in two separate places."

The Earth contained an abundance of dissolved gases; hydrogen, oxygen, nitrogen, and carbon dioxide predominated. They poured forth from the surface through the extensive volcanic activity that encircled the Earth. The hydrogen burned in the oxygen, due to the heat of the red-hot magma, from which it came, and formed water vapour. This, with the two other gases, nitrogen and carbon dioxide, formed the bulk of an atmosphere that build around the Earth, retained by its gravity. The heat of the Earth over many millennia caused the water vapour to stay in the atmosphere as a gas until the cooling of the Earth, and also the upper layers of the atmosphere, allowed clouds to form through condensation.

The water vapour condensed onto the trillions of specs of dust thrown up by the volcanoes, those suspended by convection, too light to fall back to the surface of the Earth. These clouds then shielded the surface of the Earth from direct sunlight, helping to accelerate the cooling process. The cloud layer built in thickness, as did the water droplet size, finally becoming large enough for gravity to cause rain to fall. This was, finally, the separation of water vapour in cloud form, above the Earth, from the liquid water building up on the surface below—and it was done.

So, God had made a dome of what we call atmosphere and clouds above the Earth, and it separated the water under it from the water above it. He named the dome "Sky".

Volcanism continued to encircle the Earth. The molten core bursting forth, spewing out millions upon millions of tons of material, in addition to the gases that continued to build the atmosphere. The sky, as a result, was permanently covered in cloud and laden with dust. This attenuated the sunlight falling on the surface of the Earth. As the Earth cooled more rapidly—the water vapour condensed more quickly, the formation of clouds accelerated, thus producing ever more rain. It became a quickening spiral of meteorological events that caused water to build upon the surface of the Earth, progressively covering it in an ever-deepening layer.

As the Earth continued to cool, more of the magma solidified into rocks, the oldest of these has been found in Greenland. It's a conglomerate rock, now commonly associated with a beach or a riverbed, dated at three point eight billion years old. The combination of volcanism and cooling caused a great mix of elements, and many combinations, to be randomly trapped within the thickening crust and atmosphere of the Earth. From hydrogen to fluorine, neon to argon—potassium to cobalt—nickel to krypton—rubidium to rhodium—palladium to xenon—caesium to europium—gadolinium to hafnium—tantalum to thallium—lead to thorium—protactinium and uranium—all ninety-two elements of the periodic table were present to a greater or lesser degree.

When this thickening crust became more rigid, averaging about eight miles thick at this time, it cracked into a series of what we now call tectonic plates. This was due to continuous distortion from the force of gravity exerted by the sun, moon and planets, as well as the magma's continuing turmoil from within.

Another two billion, fifty-five million, two hundred and eight thousand, nine hundred and sixty years had passed— half of all remaining time.

Evening passed and morning came—that was the second day.

Then God commanded, "Let the water below the sky come together in one place, so that land will appear."

Now had come the time in God's plan of creation, when evolution began to shape the surface of the world. Huge plumes of magma within the Earth lifted the broken crust in some areas, causing other areas to sink. The water drained away from the higher ground onto the lower ground.

Thus, some of the earth's surface rose out of the water that had covered the globe; the first of these was "Gondwanaland". Over the ensuing millennia, it grew larger until it was huge, covering a major part of the Southern Hemisphere. It was destined to be Antarctica, Australasia, South America, Africa and India.

A second area of land appeared— "Laurentia"—that also grew over time, in a mainly equatorial position. It was smaller and was to become North America, Greenland and Scotland.

Then a third area of land emerged— "Siberia"—on the opposite side of the globe; it also sat astride the equator. It became large and was destined to be most of Asia and part of Europe.

Finally, a fourth, smaller area of land arose— "Baltica"—it would become part of Asia and part of Europe.

As these four countries developed, some inland waters remained, volcanoes grew mountains and hills; their ash still filled the sky. It continued to rain; rivers of water flowed in the warmer climes, glaciers formed in colder climes, each carving-out the land spectacularly.

These landmasses moved over time—continental drift—an inch or two each year, about a mile every sixty thousand years. This movement slowly took Gondwanaland northward, bringing what were to be Africa and South America towards the equator. Laurentia drifted southeast and Siberia drifted southwest; they eventually merged by the end of this, the third day—and it was done.

He named the land "Earth" and the water, which came together, he named "Sea." And God was pleased with what He saw.

Then God commanded "Let the earth produce all kinds of plants, those that bear grain and those that bear fruit."

The prerequisites for plant growth were now in place. Water had covered and soaked the Earth's surface since the end of the Archeozoic Period. A high concentration of carbon dioxide in the atmosphere for the plants to breathe, this also produced a hot climate from the greenhouse effect of carbon dioxide. The humidity was high from excess water vapour, forming clouds, producing rain. Nutrients were present in the earth, laid down over millions of years, produced by microfossils and a combination of bacteria and blue/green algae that lived in the warm shallow waters.

The trigger for the development of plants was produced by a massive burst of radiation from a supernova. It caused a mutation, an aberration in the form of Eukaryotes, a highly organised cell nucleus, surrounded by a membrane. They became the earliest forms of fungi and seaweed, produced about one thousand, five hundred million years ago. The Eukaryotes contained chlorophyll and other pigments, allowing photosynthesis to gently commence in the overcast and somewhat gloomy light. They lacked stems, roots or leaves, but were the progenitors of today's plants.

In a very small way, the slow but steady consumption of atmospheric carbon dioxide had started; it aided the building process of plant life. In turn, through the photosynthetic process, the plants released oxygen. In this way the slow transition of our atmosphere began, carbon dioxide being replaced by oxygen. The earth had started to awaken to the filtered sunlight as the still crude Earth continued to creep towards the Cambrian Period of the Palaeozoic era. *So the earth produced all kinds of plants, and God was pleased with what He saw.*

Another half of all remaining time had passed—one billion, twenty-seven million, six hundred and four thousand, four hundred and eighty years. *Evening passed and morning came—that was the third day.*

Then God commanded "Let lights appear in the sky to separate day from night and show the time when days, seasons and years begin; they will shine in the sky to give light to the earth."

Very slowly, volcanism declined, this produced a commensurate reduction in atmospheric pollution. The release of hydrogen, oxygen and other gases also started to decline. The atmosphere was beginning to approach a state of equilibrium, the heavy overcast conditions lightened progressively and the rains helped clear the sky. Sulphur from volcanoes, consequent acid rain, the massive volume of dust that had blocked the power of the sun—all at last was in decline.

The cloud cover began to break—the sky slowly cleared, revealing the sun, the moon and the stars to the surface of the Earth. At the same time the sun itself was growing hotter, creating near tropical conditions, accelerating the photosynthesis of plant growth.

A greater differential between land and sea temperature developed, caused by direct sunlight, in turn producing stronger thermals and more powerful winds. These two factors mixing the atmospheric gases and creating more rapid evaporation altered the level of atmospheric instability. Consequently more variable meteorological cycles developed—Cumulonimbus clouds formed more rapidly, followed by periods of heavy rain that watered the plants. The growth of plant life began to accelerate dense accumulations of single cell planktonic algae and multi-cellular phytoplankton also formed, such as acritarches. This sequence of events continued throughout the Cambrian Period—*and it was done.*

So God made the two larger lights appear on Earth, *the sun to rule over the day and the moon to rule over the night; he had also made the stars appear. He had placed the lights in the sky to shine on the earth, to rule over the day and the night, and to separate light from darkness.*

Meanwhile, the lands continued to move and evolve—Gondwanaland, Laurentia and Siberia, as parts of Pangea, now began to drift apart. By the end of this, the fourth day, all three would sit astride the equator. The heat continued to produce tropical conditions, this, combined with monsoon rains, partly flooded the continents, the excess run-off water producing an overall rise in sea levels. Some regional and localised uplifting of lands followed, caused by volcanic mountain building activity.

Some of the last super-volcanoes, which had filled the sky with dust, left traces that have since been identified. The Long Valley Caldera in California, the Valles Caldera in New Mexico, the Kamchatka Caldera in Eastern Russia and the Yellowstone Caldera in Wyoming, to name but four.

A period of five hundred and thirteen million, eight hundred and two thousand, two hundred and forty years had passed, yet another half of all remaining time. God's earlier commands were growing towards maturity. And God was pleased with what He saw. *Evening passed and morning came—that was the fourth day.*

Then God commanded, "Let the water be filled with many kinds of living beings, and let the air be filled with many birds", at the start of the Ordovician Period.

Protists, unicellular organisms that were on the borderline of plants, had formed in the water, eight hundred million years ago; the first coelenterates had also evolved. Now came another tremendous burst of adaptive radiation, it mutated the Protists and coelenterates into a range of highly diversified trilobites, lampshells, graptolites and groups of gastropods.

This adaptive radiation also brought into being sea urchins, and was the origin of all five orders of starfish.

Then came a significant alteration to the evolutionary direction, when the earth passed through the radiation of a supernova, an enormous cosmic explosion. It caused the mass extinction of much marine life; the subsequent evolution showed a further change of direction.

The Silurian period saw the first jawed fishes appear—eurypterids, chondrichthyans and Osteichthyes. The coral reefs that had built-up over aeons of time resulted in the formation of warm lagoons—in these, ammonites and the first amphibian tetrapod evolved.

A second culling of marine life occurred from a further exposure to cosmic radiation, redirecting the evolutionary path yet again. Tetrapods like Pederpes, the first fish to crawl onto land emerged, then the first reptiles appeared. Graptolites became extinct, but early sharks and bony fish started to thrive. Trilobites finally died out and early reptiles started to diversify, one being the progenitor of archaeopteryx, the first of the birds. Other reptiles were the forefathers of the dinosaurs that appeared in the Triassic Period.

So God created the great sea monsters, and all kinds of creatures that live in the water and all kinds of birds. And God was pleased with what he saw. He blessed them all and told the creatures that live in the water to reproduce and to fill the sea and he told the birds to increase in number.

While the development of marine life was evolving, the same adaptive radiation had also caused plant life to diversify.

First, spores resembling those of modern plants began to emerge. Then in the Silurian period the first vascular plants grew, such as club mosses and yellow-green algae. There was progressive colonisation of the land by these plants and they became as big as today's trees. Ferns and the first seeded plants also appeared.

Plant life became extremely verdant in the Carboniferous Period, many millions of generations of plants, over millions of years. The deposits from this vegetation formed into anthracite in the lowland swaps during the Jurassic Period. This fantastic growth of vegetation slowed as the level of carbon dioxide in the atmosphere diminished. The decaying material went on to produce bituminous coal, lignite and late in the period, brown coal and peat. During the process of decomposition, the vegetation also produced huge pockets of methane gas.

Then modern families of conifers, except pines, came into being, and thrived in the drier conditions. Gymnosperm grew to dominance in the Triassic Period and ferns remained important. Forests of cycads, conifers and gingkoes spread even further across the lands.

The second burst of adaptive radiation also brought about a further change in vegetation. Deciduous and broad-leaved trees appeared and came to dominate many areas of land, also the first grasses appeared.

As plant life evolved, so did the landmasses of the world. Baltica moved towards the equator, closer to Laurentia. The continent of Gondwanaland on the other hand, moved south, became much colder, causing glaciers to form. Some of these grew to within thirty degrees of the equator, they became so widespread that they caused the overall sea level to fall.

Baltica finally collided with Laurasia and Gondwanaland narrowed, the continental drift of the landmasses and the progressive warming of the seas, began to have a further climatic effect through the development of ocean currents. Finally, in the late Carboniferous Period and early Permian Period Laurasia and Gondwanaland finally collided to form the super-continent of Pangaea. Siberia subsequently collided with Pangaea, which started the formation of the Ural Mountains late in the Permian Period.

At the start of the Triassic Period, almost all of the earth's land surfaces were joined together. The huge landmass virtually covered one side of the world. This resulted in very arid conditions for large areas of land that were far from water. The great ocean of Panthalassa covered the rest of the globe.

There were profound climatic differences from region to region, but as time passed the world warmed once more, causing the heavy glaciation in the south to slowly melt, ocean levels rose again.

Once more, half of all the remaining time had passed, another two hundred and fifty-six million, nine hundred and one thousand, one hundred and twenty years.

Evening passed and morning came—that was the fifth day.

Day six of creation was markedly different, a day that lasted through no less than fifteen steps of time. The first six steps ran from the Triassic Period to the Pliocene Epoch. God intervened three times to ensure that evolution produced the kind of animal He wanted us to be—a particular form to fashion and become humankind.

Once humankind existed, the second part of day six consisted of nine further, ever-quickening steps of time, in the Pleistocene Epoch. God intervened four more times to ensure that the evolution of humankind met His purpose, the point at which He could create Mankind.

Step one of day six was perhaps the most dramatic, it came during the transition from the Permian to the Triassic Period. It saw the greatest mass extinction of all time, around two hundred and fifty million years ago. Literally a seismic event, its magnitude so great, it caused the extinction of 90% of all living creatures. It has become known as the time of 'Great Dying'.

It was caused by a huge asteroid impact, it produced a massive crater, one hundred and twenty-five miles in diameter, called the 'Bedout High'. It hit an area just off the coast of southern Pangea, an area that is now off the northwest coast of Australia. It caused a ripple effect in the Earth's crust creating volcanoes and opening up large pockets of methane gas. The atmosphere filled with debris, the sun dimmed, vegetation declined dramatically and methane gas poisoned the atmosphere.

The fittest 10% that survived brought another change in the direction of evolution. Teleosts came into being, the dominant fish group of today, and enormous marine reptiles such as ichthyosaurs and plesiosaurs. Thecodonts became the flying reptiles known as pterosaurs; the era of dinosaurs had emerged. Turtles, marine lizards and crocodiles that had been thriving declined significantly during the Jurassic Period. Dinosaurs diversified to the point where archaeopteryx, the first true bird appeared, it had well-developed wings and a body covered with feathers. Teleosts also underwent a dramatic change, producing herrings, carp, eels, cod and perch; they all thrived during the Cretaceous Period. In addition the most spectacular vertebrates appeared—marine plesiosaurs, giant turtles and the newly evolved mosasaurs. The sea creatures, commanded on day five, were now a reality.

The penultimate moves that created today's geography were also taking place. Rifting occurred between Laurasia and Gondwanaland, initially separating Southern Europe from Africa. Pangea tore in two, opening up what is now the Central Atlantic. South America started to separate from Africa to begin to form the South Atlantic. What was to become India separated from Antarctica. The final phase began when Greenland tore away from the North American and the European parts of Pangea.

One hundred and twenty million, four hundred and fifty thousand, five hundred and sixty years had passed during step one of day six, another half-life of time.

Then God commanded "Let the earth produce all kinds of animal life: domestic and wild, large and small"—this was the beginning of step two.

The cataclysmic events in step one had led the chosen genes into producing the coelacanth. It was past fish, part animal; it formed the bridge, the transition that took place from fish to animals.

The very first of the mammalian groups emerged from this, it was an early lemur like primate—Adapidae— evolution had produced the first step in the animal kingdom that would lead to humankind—*and it was done.*

During this time, when rifting in the Jurassic Period had separated Europe from Africa, Iberia was left in between, this now started to converge on Europe.

Sub-tropical flora came as far north as present day Southern England. Modern families of flowering plants evolved, and the Palaeocene Epoch saw the emergence of today's grasses.

As the end of step two on day six approached, some sixty-five million years ago, a second cataclysmic event occurred. It was of lesser proportions, but nonetheless it caused the extinction of about 60% of all living creatures on Earth, including the dinosaurs. It was caused by a meteor impact in Chicxulub, an area in Mexico's Yucatan Peninsula. It produced another supersonic shock wave that circled the Earth and brought about similar effects to the Bedout High, albeit less severe. Step two of day six lasted sixty-four million, two hundred and twenty-five thousand, two hundred and eighty years. The first of the land animals had been created and another half of time had passed.

In step three of day six, the pace of animal evolution began to quicken. Hoofed animal groups emerged early pigs, camels, hippopotami, deer, and antelopes, then came cattle, horses, tapirs and rhinoceroses. Anteaters, sloths, armadillos, elephants, whales and rodents followed. Early carnivorous animals also evolved such as cats, dogs, bears, racoons, hyenas, civets and weasels. Finally dwarf lemurs and eye-ayes, which were squirrel-like lemurs emerged.

The Oligocene and Eocene Epochs saw the development of the present range of trees that began to give the land a distinctly modern appearance. Additionally, the continued development and growth of grasses enabled them to invade open country and withstand heavy grazing.

The Indian tectonic plate had continued northward and began to collide with Eurasia, as it was now called, leading to the formation of the Himalayas over the ensuing 30 million years. The Eurasian Basin in the Far East opened as the final fragmentation of that end of the Eurasian continent occurred. Iberia finally collided with Europe to begin the formation of the Pyrenean Mountains over the following 20 million years and Australia separated from both South America and the Antarctic continent.

A further thirty-two million, one hundred and twelve thousand, six hundred and forty years of day six had passed, yet another half of remaining time.

Step four of day six saw the start of God's final preparation to produce that special kind of animal with the irradiation of mammals from another supernova. Tarsiformes then emerged, looking like a lemuroid kind of monkey. These evolved into Tarsiers, a nocturnal primate with huge eyes, long hind legs, and digits ending in pads to facilitate climbing. Anthropoids appeared that were early higher primates called Sakis. Further animal evolution brought into being Marmosets and Tamarins—monkeys with clawed digits, and Gibbons which were small anthropoid apes.

Owls and spiders had also appeared and all orders of birds were now completed.

The climate deteriorated, the polar regions cooled, significantly less rain fell, and by the end of the Oligocene Epoch glaciation had once more caused sea levels to drop appreciably. Forests shrank, but herbaceous plants appeared and grasses continued to spread, becoming hardier.

The main phase of Alpine Mountain building began and Red Sea rifting started in East Africa, these were the first hesitant step that ultimately led to the formation of Africa, the Red Sea and the Persian Gulf. The Himalayas rose higher as India pushed further into Asia. Then further movement brought progress in the formation of the Mediterranean, so that it began to look like the sea we know it today.

This forth step of day six took sixteen million, fifty-six thousand, three hundred and twenty years, yet another half of all remaining time. Day's six fifth step of time saw the slow emergence of yet more new animal groups including frogs, snakes, mice and rats.

The flora developed to the point where it looked much as today and phytoplankton finally died out.

The uplifting of the Isthmus of Panama began; it would bridge the gap between North and South America and finally separate the Atlantic and Pacific Oceans. Little seemed to happen; the final detail of evolution lay hidden, yet it lasted eight million and twenty-eight thousand, one hundred and sixty years, again half of remaining time.

By the sixth step of day six, over two billion years had passed to bring about the final consolidation of God's earlier commands to create fish, birds and animals, including what we call 'Chad Tomah', the immediate forebear of the Hominids. This Epoch also saw the emergence of mammoths.

So God made them all, and He was pleased with what He saw.

The Isthmus of Panama, finally joining North and South America was completed during the Pliocene Epoch. The sea levels started to rise again as the Earth warmed and the geography of the world, its continents, oceans and seas were virtually, as we know them today.

God's earlier commands had been fulfilled. Earth was ready for the penultimate phase of His plan.

So then, in step seven of day six, God said, "and now we will make human beings; they will be like us and resemble us. They will have power over the fish, the birds and all the animals, domestic and wild, large and small."

The higher primates, Gorillas, Chimpanzee, Gibbons and Orangutan followed from this command. From these creatures emerged the first generation of Hominids, Australopithecus, about three million four hundred thousand years ago.

So God created the first human beings making them to be (come) like himself.

This seventh step of time, that brought the creation of mankind, lasted just two million, seven thousand, and forty-two years. It was again, half of all remaining time.

Christopher's notes on day eight could not be found—we decided to move on. This saw the emergence of Homo Erectus.

By the end of step eight, also the end of the Pleistocene Epoch, many of the large animals, such as mammoths and giant beavers had died out.

Another one million and three thousand, five hundred and twenty years had passed—another half of remaining time.

By step nine of day six, there had been some eighteen cold periods on the earth—six had been quite severe ice ages. Now, four further ice ages came upon the Earth in more rapid succession. The first of these, the Gunz ice age, came in step nine, about eight hundred thousand years ago. This brought severe hardship to Homo Erectus, causing the demise of many and the survival of the few—the fittest.

Another five hundred and one thousand, seven hundred and sixty years had passed—the ever-quickening half-life of time.

The second of these ice ages, the Mindel, came in step ten of time, about four hundred thousand years ago. It brought a further thinning-out of the population; again it was the survival of the fittest.

Two hundred and fifty thousand, eight hundred and eighty years passed. The ice age forcing Homo Erectus to use his brain, as well as his physical ability, to survive. Homo Erectus was evolving and gaining in intellect.

The interval between the ice ages allowed for recovery in the numbers of the population. The third, the Riss ice age, came in step eleven, some two hundred thousand years ago. It was a repeat of the process of human development, but this time it produced a key genetic mutation, the FOXp2 gene that was to give humankind their unique speech capability.

This further half-life of time took one hundred and twenty-five thousand, four hundred and forty years.

The ice age selection process brought about very considerable human development, including a further increase in brain size. A consolidation period was provided in step twelve, to physically strengthen Homo Erectus after three successive ice age privations, as well as a recovery in population numbers. There was no ice age, it was a time for humankind to develop its newfound skills, further improve its ability to adapt and survive, to eventually become master of the fish, the birds, and all the wild animals.

This period lasted another half-life of time, sixty-two thousand, and seven hundred and twenty years.

At the beginning of step thirteen, some ten thousand pairs of Homo Erectus were spread across central Africa. They were the offspring of those who had elected to move towards the warmer equatorial regions as the ice ages had spread from the poles. Of the remainder who had not migrated down into Africa, most had died, but those few pairs that had survived the severe conditions were much tougher. The lack of ice age allowed the latter in particular to develop their physical stamina and skills still further. During the thirty-one thousand, three hundred and sixty years of step thirteen; all the survivors became, to varying degrees, a very high order of animal indeed.

At the beginning of step fourteen, the last ice age arrived, the Wurm, thirty-one thousand years ago. It tested, developed or culled humankind one last time, producing the finalised human stock. Homo Erectus had become transformed into modern humankind—Homo Sapiens—about thirty thousand years ago.

As the Wurm ice age receded and the earth warmed once more, Homo Sapiens slowly spread up through Kenya, Ethiopia, and Egypt into the eastern Mediterranean. They later continued on into Persia, and across southern Asia as far as the Indian sub-continent.

Homo Sapiens was still corporeal, as had been Hominids and Homo Erectus before them, but now they began to show signs of creativity in the form of carvings and crude art in cave drawings, some dating back twenty-eight thousand years.

He created them male and female, blessed them, and said, "Have many children, so that your descendants will live all over the earth and bring it under control. I am putting you in charge of the fish, the birds, and all the wild animals. I have provided all kinds of grain and all kinds of fruit for you to eat; but for all the wild animals and for all the birds I have provided grass and leafy plants for food"—and it was done.

In the fifteenth and final step of day six, which on mankind's calendar now coincides with 11,766 to 3,926 BC, Homo Sapiens progressively became more social, language was evolving, and they learnt to farm and hunt in groups. Eleven thousand years ago, circa 9,000 BC, they had started to live in small communities, farmsteads, hamlets and villages. Evidence of permanent settlements has been found in the Near East and North Africa. There is also evidence of the domestication of animals as well as the growing of wheat and barley. In the thousand years, 8,350-7,350 BC, Jericho, the first walled town in the world, was slowly build up.

Homo Sapiens had, by now, migrated as far as China, where there is evidence that rice cultivation started around 7,250 BC. Anthropologists have also found traces of experiments made with copper ore in Anatolia around 7,000 BC.

Homo Sapiens was farming in Greece and the Aegean c 6,500 BC and a second city—Catal Huyuk—was built in Turkey (6,250-5,600 BC) where the first samples of pottery and woollens have been found. Homo Sapiens spread up the Danube into Hungary, c 5,500 BC and then along the Mediterranean coast to France, c 5,000 BC. They colonised the alluvial plains of Mesopotamia, practiced irrigation and formed agricultural settlements in Egypt around the same time. The migration continued into Germany, the Low Countries and Britain c 4,500 BC.

Due to climate change, desiccation of the Sahara began c 4,000 BC. It divided the residual North African population in two, some were driven north, inhabiting the Mediterranean coast, while others moved progressively south once more.

In the last year of step fifteen—3, 926 BC—there came the moment that God chose to create Mankind, *he breathed life-giving breath into his nostrils and the man began to live.*

This was the gift of a spiritual principle to human beings. The human body sharing in the dignity of "the image of God." A human body now animated by a soul. A creation that signifies that mankind is enabled to have a spiritual dimension to share with God, if he so chooses. Mankind now had, for the very first time, an awareness of the existence of God.

A later chapter in the Book of Genesis addresses this event, saying *He created them male and female, blessed then, and named then "Mankind".*

They were no longer simply human—they now had a conscience and a soul. They could determine right from wrong, in addition to the power of logical and original thought—the ability to choose the path they would follow. They could plan and decide their own destiny. God also said, "This is just the beginning of what they are going to do. Soon they will be able to do anything they want!"

They would gain dominion over the whole world and mankind's horizons would become almost limitless. Mankind was no longer just a sophisticated animal, no longer corporeal, mankind was now able to live, not just exist!

After two hundred and fifty-six million, eight hundred and ninety-seven thousand, one hundred and ninety-four years of day six, the whole of creation was complete. It was also the end of the twentieth step of time. God looked at everything he had made, and He was very pleased. Evening passed and morning came—that was the sixth day.

And so the whole universe was completed. By the seventh day God finished what he had been doing and stopped working. He blessed the seventh day and set it apart as a special day, because by that day he had completed his creation and stopped working. And that is how the universe was created.

From the moment when there was nothing, from the instant when God chose to create a singularity, eight billion, two hundred and twenty million, eight hundred and thirty-five thousand eight hundred and fifty years had passed, just over 99.9% of all time.

So, it came to pass that Adam and Eve entered the twenty-first step of time—3926 BC to 6 BC—recorded as the first of mankind. The thirty-nine books of the Old Testament, the remainder of Genesis to the prophet Malachi, tell about the life of mankind in all its colourful detail. The sixty-one generations, ten from Adam and Eve to Noah, nine from Noah to Abraham and in the first chapter of St Matthew's Gospel, the forty-two generations from Abraham to the birth of Christ in 6 BC.